Trapped on the top floor—no elevator, no cell phone. The man you thought you'd never see again walks in the door, looking sexy as ever, but not offering any reason for missing your planned rendezvous seven months ago....

You're seething—from the heat or from the man, you're not sure which. You just know you've got to keep your lips sealed...or else you'll give away what the darkness is hiding.

And then, the first contraction hits....

WHERE WERE YOU WHEN THE LIGHTS WENT OUT?

Dear Reader,

I can vaguely remember the great blackout of 1965, when most of New York went dark for the night. My family was at home when it hit, but some people were trapped in interesting places!

That's how it is for the three couples in this exciting new trilogy that asks the question "Where Were You When the Lights Went Out?" It's Fourth of July, in the midst of a torrid heat wave, when a blackout darkens much of the West Coast. You're not going to believe the places and situations these couples get trapped in! Be sure you don't miss any of the action in the subsequent titles by Linda Randall Wisdom and Jacqueline Diamond.

My sister and I spent our blackout night listening to the Beatles on the radio. Trust me, though, these couples make much better use of their time!

Regards,

Debra Matteucci
Senior Editor & Editorial Coordinator
Harlequin Books
300 E. 42nd St.
New York, NY 10017

MARY ANNE WILSON

NINE MONTHS LATER...

Harlequin Books

TORONTO • NEW YORK • LONDON
AMSTERDAM • PARIS • SYDNEY • HAMBURG
STOCKHOLM • ATHENS • TOKYO • MILAN
MADRID • WARSAW • BUDAPEST • AUCKLAND

ISBN 0-373-16637-0

NINE MONTHS LATER...

This edition published by arrangement with Harlequin Books S.A.

® and TM are trademarks of the publisher. Trademarks indicated with
® are registered in the United States Patent and Trademark Office, the
Canadian Trade Marks Office and in other countries.

Printed in U.S.A.

Chapter One

Late October
San Diego, California

"What a miserable day." Dylan Bradford frowned as she looked out the rain-streaked windshield of her old BMW coupe. "It hardly ever rains in San Diego this time of year, it's only four o'clock in the afternoon, and it's almost as dark as night."

"Dylan, rain happens. Clouds make things dark. So what?" Her younger sister, Tori, shifted in the passenger seat of the car and spoke with annoying condescension. "You know, when you're pregnant, little things don't bother you so much. You focus more. Everything just sort of falls into place. It's wonderful." She sighed. "Your skin clears up. You have all this energy after the first couple of months, and you get a sense of peace that's indescribable. Life seems just right. Perfect. And rain just doesn't matter."

Dylan loved her sister, but as she drove onto the main street that led toward the shopping center near the older section of the city, her nerves were beginning to bunch at the back of her neck.

The traffic was moving at a snail's pace, all but snarled to a standstill by the drizzling rain. And Tori hadn't stopped talking about the joys of impending parenthood since Dylan had picked her up at her doctor's office to give her a ride to the mall.

"Rain is rain, and you're pregnant and fat and happy," Dylan muttered as she flipped on her headlights. "Can't we talk about something else for a while?"

"I'm not fat—just eight months pregnant. And I wish I could get you to understand exactly how all this feels." Tori barely took a breath before launching into a well-worn refrain sprinkled liberally with "I love you and only want the best for you" and punctuated with "You don't know what you're missing." Then she said smugly, "And you know, people think your sex drive just goes into hibernation, but believe me, it doesn't."

That was all Dylan needed to hear about right now—her pregnant sister's sex life—especially when she couldn't figure out how Tori and her husband, Allan, could even reach each other around Tori's belly. She flexed her hands on the steering wheel and took a deep breath to help keep her voice even. "Okay, okay. I don't know what I'm missing and never will." As she swung the car to the right to get into the lane that led toward the front of the enclosed shopping mall, she added to herself, *Thank goodness*.

A screech of tires came at the same time a horn blared somewhere behind the car. "Haven't you ever heard of turn signals?" Tori gasped.

Dylan shrugged, keeping her eyes ahead on a black Mercedes sedan that glistened with rain clinging to its highly waxed finish. "I had plenty of room." She couldn't resist a touch of sarcasm. "Where's all this peace you were talking about?"

"I knew I should have taken a taxi," Tori muttered.

"I saved you twenty dollars, and you're almost there, so relax."

"I'd like to make it to my next natural childbirth class, at least."

"Don't be so dramatic." Dylan sighed as she squinted through the streaked windshield to try and spot a traffic lane that would get her as close as possible to the entrance of the Spanish-style mall. "With all this 'natural childbirth' talk, I just bet when it comes right down to giving birth, you'll be yelling for drugs after the first good pain."

"Drugs aren't good for the baby."

Dylan glanced at her sister and couldn't resist saying, "They don't call it 'labor' for nothing."

But her words were lost when Tori grabbed at her arm with one hand and pointed ahead of them with the other as she gasped, "Watch where you're going!"

Dylan looked ahead and jammed on her brakes. The tires squealed on the wet pavement and held, mere inches away from the black Mercedes that had stopped in front of her. As the car settled, Dylan muttered, "Crazy driver," and jerked her arm out of Tori's death grip as she glared at the expensive car with its tinted windows.

She could vaguely make out the silhouette of the driver, a man who appeared to be looking back at her in his rearview mirror. But the rain and the tinted glass made seeing his features impossible. Actually, she wasn't at all sure she wanted to see his expression too clearly right then. "What does he think this is? A parking lot?"

"He's paying attention to what he's doing," Tori said as she sank back in the seat again. "Unlike certain people with a terrible driving record, who are so preoccupied with some old buildings that we almost ran into the back of that very expensive car."

"He stopped without warning," Dylan insisted as she glanced at her sister.

She and Tori had always had a love-hate relationship, starting with the moment when Dylan had seen her new baby sister for the first time. She'd looked at the red and wrinkled newborn and wondered why her parents had bothered with another child. And when she and Tori had been growing up, she'd figured out that part of the reason for their fights had been that they were as different as night and day.

Victoria Julianna—with her light blue eyes, pale, freckled skin and deep coppery hair cut very short around her face—was what people would call gamine and cute. Dylan Briar, named after some obscure Irish poet, was darker, with deep blue eyes, long, almost raven-black hair she wore in low twists or ponytails, and skin that was tanned all year around, sun or not.

Tori as a child had been all ruffles and lace and dolls and stuffed animals. Now Tori, as an adult, had a husband, a home and a baby on the way, and she'd found what she called over and over again "real happiness."

But Dylan as a child had hated bows and ribbons, instead choosing jeans and shirts, and ignoring dolls, she'd cornered the market on building blocks and Erector sets.

Tori had read poetry, shopped incessantly for clothes and fallen in love every ten minutes until she met Allan and had fallen in love forever. Meanwhile, Dylan had dated off and on, really didn't have time to consider being in love, had a degree in architecture, and nurtured a dream of having her own architectural restoration firm.

She was so close to that dream right now. And Tori had been absolutely right: Her mind had been on some old buildings about two miles from here, buildings that had at one time been in the heart of San Diego. But they had fallen into disrepair and been abandoned. Now she had the chance to change all that.

A week ago, she had put in a bid on a contract with the city to restore those buildings as a new business complex. And if she got the contract, she knew she would be able to start her own company and, yes, she would be close to real happiness.

"*This* person is thinking about a contract," she admitted. "And about a new business that I could have." She eased her car forward again, keeping a bit of distance between herself and the black Mercedes.

"And you're going to quit your perfectly good job at Barnes and Blazer," Tori said with unflappable calm.

The mention of her job only made her neck tighten more. "I never wanted to work for anyone like Aaron Barnes and John Blazer, but I had to. I have to, until I can start my own company. Then I'm out of there. I'll take a chance, and if I get this contract to redo the four Santa Clare buildings, I can make Bradford Associates a reality." She took a deep, tight breath. "Can't you understand why I want that?"

"I understand how much you want this business of yours, how in love you are with the idea of being your own boss."

"If that's love, it's safer than any sex is." Dylan tried to ease things with the forced joke. "*And* I'm guaranteed not to end up with a huge stomach and have to come all the way down here to find a black nightgown for one last fling with my husband before sex is banned altogether."

The driver in the black car ahead of them glanced back at Dylan in the rearview mirror, and she barely killed the urge to wave to him or give him some other kind of hand gesture. He seemed to be checking his mirror every few seconds now.

"I hate to think of a whole month without being able to make love," Tori lamented, choosing to ignore the sarcasm.

"You *can* have sex now, can't you?" Dylan asked as they neared the main lanes that led to the entrance of the mall.

"Of course, and I just want to look good tonight."

She glanced at her sister who was gently patting her stomach. "Are you sure? I mean, you're so...so big."

"Very sure," Tori replied frowning at Dylan. Then, out of the blue, she said, "I thought when you hit thirty, you'd be different."

Dylan was taken aback by the reference to her age, because she seldom thought about it. Apparently it meant less to her than to her sister. "I won't be thirty for over eight months, and what does my age have to do with anything?"

Tori raised an eyebrow at her sister. "You're not a kid anymore, Dylan."

"Since I'm only three years older than you are, I'm not exactly ancient."

"Of course, you aren't," she said as she patted her stomach absentmindedly. "But you need to get a life."

"That kid's going to be born with a flat head if you don't quit patting it all the time. And I've got a life."

"Sure you do."

"I've got a career I love, and I've got you and Mom and Dad and Allan and—" she waved one hand in the direction of Tori's stomach "—the kid when it comes."

"You know the baby's a boy and his name's Allan James and we're going to call him A.J. He's not an 'it' or 'the kid.'"

"Okay. And I've got a life," Dylan said as she drove slowly forward and the sky grew darker and darker.

"How about that guy you were dating—Arnold or Andrew or something, the policeman?"

"Andrew, and he was a security specialist, not a cop," she said, barely able to remember what the man looked like. "And what about him?"

"Well, you haven't mentioned him for a while."

"Because he's got a life, too."

"But not with you?"

"Bingo. We aren't going to get into the one about a special man in my life, and my biological clock ticking, are we?"

"You know I admire your drive and intelligence, and that I don't believe that a woman needs a man to be happy."

There'd been men in her life, Dylan thought. Men like Andrew, coming in and out, but never a man who made her forget about the other things going on in her life. There had never been anyone who swept her off her feet the way her brother-in-law had done with Tori. And no one who had ever been close to being as important to her as her dreams. "Thanks for that, at least."

"I mean it. It's just—"

"You want me to be happy?"

"Exactly."

"I've got a news flash for you, Tori. I'll be happy when I get that contract and can start my own company." When she heard Tori take a deep breath, readying for another verbal volley, she quickly diverted her with "Are you sure you want me to just drop you off like this?"

"I need to buy the nightgown and go home to get ready. Go ahead and look through your buildings for the hundredth time. A.J. and I will do just fine."

Dylan wished she and Tori could just talk the way she was certain most sisters did, without always seeming to end up on opposite ends of any issue. She loved Tori, despite everything, and as she turned to her sister, she caught a flash of red out of the corner of her eye. She realized the glow was from brake lights ahead at the same moment she knew it was too late to stop herself from running into the back of the black Mercedes.

COOPER REEVES CURSED the rain, the traffic and the car Brokaw had loaned to him while he cooled his heels for the next few days. Actually, his mood had been bordering on black since Brokaw had told him the final hurdle to getting a five year contract with his company would take another two or three days. Only then could he head for Spain and start the testing on the prototype cars that were being developed for Brokaw's company under tight security.

But he wasn't good at waiting; never had been, never would be. Always wanting instant gratification, that was what someone had told him. He had an addiction to it, and that was why he pushed the limits on everything in his life. For the next few days, though, he had no choice but to wait. So he could either stay in his hotel room or drive around San Diego, a city he'd never been in before, in a luxury car that looked great, but was annoyingly temperamental.

The luxury car seemed to be insulted by the rain— rain that Coop had been told was very unusual for this time of year in Southern California. The engine ground roughly after each puddle, and threatened to stall at any given time if the water was more than an inch deep.

He raked his fingers through his sandy brown hair as he looked through the rain-streaked windows, and a low oath cut through the stillness inside the car. Somehow he'd ended up in a lane of traffic that he'd expected would take him toward the freeway but instead had funnelled him into an expansive parking area for what looked like an enclosed shopping mall.

He checked in both directions and knew he was well and truly caught in the traffic. There was no option but to go with the flow, then cut off after the mall and hope he would be heading west and away from the traffic by then. He eased through another puddle, but obviously didn't slow enough when he felt the engine of the Mercedes protest the wet invasion with a shudder and a miss. He quickly put the transmission into neutral, hit the brakes with one foot and pressed the accelerator a bit with his right foot.

As he tried to keep the engine going, he heard the screech of tires behind him and glanced quickly in the rearview mirror in time to see a small BMW behind him braking so hard, the nose of the car was tilting down toward the pavement. It shuddered to a stop inches from the back of the Mercedes, then settled.

He could see a woman who was no more than a blur behind the rain-streaked windshield of the BMW. Although he'd never subscribed to the theory of "woman driver" inferiority, right then he had his doubts about the driver behind him. She looked as if she was talking to a woman alongside her, using her hands to make a point, and it was apparent that driving had a very low priority right then.

He slipped the Mercedes into gear again, felt the engine even out, and as he eased forward, a glance in the mirror showed him that the BMW was right behind him. And the woman was still talking to the person by her. He looked ahead, anxious to escape, but all he saw was a long line of cars, four abreast. So he inched forward in the rain, kept his eyes on the car behind him, and wished he was anywhere but here.

Right then, the Mercedes sabotaged that wish. As he drove slowly through a drainage crease almost in front of the entrance, water splashed up around the car, and with a shudder and a ping, the engine died. As he hit the brakes and muttered a disgusted "Swell," he caught a flash of motion behind him.

One look and he knew there was nothing he could do to stop the BMW that was coming at him. And there was no surprise when the car finally ran into his back end.

He'd had accidents before—God knew, he'd had more than his share and had always walked away in one piece. This was actually a minor collision, but the contact was jarring, snapping him forward against the restraint of the seat belt at his shoulder and middle. Then the world stilled, the rain beat down and Coop uttered a curse that vibrated in the car as he jammed the gearshift into Park.

He got out into the surprisingly warm rain, and before he could even turn and look behind him, he could feel his hair being drenched and his chambray shirt clinging to his skin. He glanced at the cars behind him lined up all the way to the main street, then he looked at the red BMW intimately entwined with the back of his car.

The telltale blue-green trickle of antifreeze mingled with the water on the pavement, and steam hissed out of the BMW's hood. As horns sounded all around, the driver's door of the BMW opened and right then, Coop knew how wrong he'd been about San Diego. He'd told Jeb Brokaw, the negotiator for his contract, that the city was boring and dull. But no city with a woman like the driver of the BMW could ever be written off that lightly.

She was tall, maybe five foot ten or so, five or six inches shorter than his own height. As she stared at her car in horror, he admired her dark, almost-ebony hair, which was caught in a simple twist with loose tendrils that clung, rain dampened, to lightly tanned skin.

As she turned toward him, he was confronted with a delicate beauty, enhanced by little or no makeup—high cheekbones, a finely shaped jawline, full lips, and blue eyes that were so dark they appeared almost navy, their long lashes spiked with moisture. Her beige silk shirt was getting soaked, practically turning into a second skin, clinging suggestively to firm breasts and even exposing the lace of her bra.

She jumped sharply when a flash of cold white lightning cut through the sky followed quickly by a crash of thunder. The sound of her voice was heavenly when she breathed, "Oh, my gosh," as the rolling sound faded and was almost drowned out by the shrill protest of car horns.

Her car hissing in the steady rain, she turned her eyes back to it and muttered, "It's ruined."

"I'd say it's not going anywhere," he replied as he moved closer to her and caught a hint of some perfume—a light, delicate scent—in the moist air.

When he spoke, she turned the full impact of her gaze on him, and he could literally feel his breath catch in his chest. God, she was beautiful, with rain falling all around her, and she had a sensuality about her that was as unstudied as it was potent. When lightning flashed again, its glow bathed her palely, and the total effect of this woman on him was as unexpected as her next words: "She's pregnant!"

"What?" He wasn't at all sure he'd heard her right, over the blare of horns and the faint sound of a siren somewhere nearby.

She moved quickly, and before he knew what she was doing, she grabbed his arm, almost dragging him back toward the open door of her car. "My sister, she's pregnant, and she's only got a month to go!"

As she spoke, her words spilling out one over the other, he went with her without a fight, all the while intensely aware of her hand on his forearm. Through the wet material, the heat of her touch seemed to brand his skin. At the open door she leaned into the car and let him go so suddenly he almost stumbled forward. In that moment, he was left with the sight of her hips and dark slacks getting soaked so that the fabric clung to her long legs.

Before he could fully absorb the images before him or deal with his instant reactions to them, she moved back out into the rain. She turned to him, her voice filled with urgency as she demanded, "What are you doing just standing there? Call the police or an ambulance or something, for heaven's sake!"

Coop backed up just a bit to get some precious distance between himself and the power that this woman seemed to possess with her mere presence. He touched the top of the open car door, thankful for the cool dampness of the metal and the chance to bend down to look inside. He found another woman in the passenger seat—a very pregnant woman. But she wasn't clutching her stomach, nor did she appear to be in any pain. And thank God, there was no blood.

The driver suddenly gripped his arm again with surprising strength, her voice right by his ear. And as she spoke, he literally felt the warmth of her breath against his neck, and her light perfume seemed to flood over him. "My sister's pregnant, and she needs help."

"I'm fine," the woman in the car said as she fiddled with her seat belt. "Honestly, I'm just—"

"Don't move," the woman holding Coop said quickly. "Tori, please, just sit still. Don't move."

He pulled back, and the hold on him was gone. But as he straightened, he found himself facing the driver with less than two feet separating them. "She says she's all right," he told her. "And there's no blood."

The finely arched eyebrows drew together in a dark frown. "What are you, an obstetrician? She's pregnant, and we just had a horrible accident."

Before he could refute her description of a fender bender as a "horrible accident," two uniformed men came rushing up. While one of them went behind the cars and began to try and funnel the line of traffic behind them to the left, the other man approached Coop and the driver. "Everyone all right, here?"

The rain was steady, warm and misty all around, and Coop swiped at his face. "We're fine, but—"

"We're *not* fine," the dark-haired woman said as she turned her back to Coop and faced the guard. "My sister's pregnant, and I need to get her to the hospital right away."

The guard, who was little more than a teenager in a uniform, went pale. "She's going to have her baby?"

"I don't know. I hope not, but we've had an accident and she could be in real trouble."

The kid darted a look at Coop. "Your wife—?"

"No," he said quickly. "I'm the one in the front car." He motioned into the BMW. "She's the one who's pregnant and she says she's fine."

The blue-eyed woman flashed Coop a dark glare, before she turned back to the guard. "Just get us to the hospital. Doctor's Memorial. It's not far, and—"

"We...we'll do what we can, but the traffic..." Rain dripped off his uniform hat and made him look pathetically ineffective.

"You've got a walkie-talkie," she said, motioning to a unit on his belt. "Call someone."

"Oh, sure, yeah, I'll call someone," he said with a touch more conviction.

Coop looked at the snarled traffic behind them, then at the woman beside the BMW. The rain was making her look almost waiflike and he killed a startling impulse to reach out and touch her. Then she swiped at her face, and he noticed that there were no rings on her left hand. When she turned back to him, he braced himself as he felt a response to her that shook him to the core.

"Can't you do something?" she asked in a softer, almost-pleading tone, her voice laced with a touch of huskiness that ran riot over his nerves.

One of his credos in a life that was isolated by design was to never get involved. And one of the last things he wanted anywhere, anytime, was to be put in a position of helping some pregnant lady. But even as he thought he should just show his papers for the car and get out of there, he was pinned by wide, deep blue eyes. Drops of rain fell from the spiked lashes, and her tongue darted out to touch the water that clung to her pale pink lips.

He took a deep breath, then jumped in with both feet. "What do you want me to do for you?" he asked, having all sorts of answers of his own to that particular question.

He saw her take a shuddering breath, which moved the clinging silk suggestively over her breasts, and he was more than a bit thankful for the slight chill of the dampening rain. "Your car," she said quickly. "It's driveable and you're up front. You can drive us to the hospital."

"But it keeps stalling. It's allergic to water. That's why I stopped in front of you. This rain—"

"It's going to take too long for an ambulance to get here and my car's not driveable. You can at least try to get your car going, can't you?"

He hesitated. He knew driving a pregnant woman to the hospital was the decent thing to do, if he could do it. But even as he nodded and agreed, he knew that his motives weren't even close to decent. "If I can get it started, I'll drive you and your sister to the hospital."

The guard looked relieved as the woman just inches from Coop whispered a heartfelt, "Thank you."

Coop faced the fact that he didn't deserve thanks. He wasn't any Good Samaritan.

He'd been dreading killing time in San Diego until the security check was complete. Then suddenly, on a gray, rainy day in October, with angry motorists blaring their horns, he'd found what looked like the perfect diversion until the security clearance was done. And that diversion had ebony hair, deep blue eyes, and a sensuality that was overwhelming.

And he didn't even know her name.

Chapter Two

Dylan didn't care about her car. She'd left it sitting in the parking lane in the rain, waiting for a tow truck to take it to a body shop. She didn't care that she was soaked to the skin, and that her suede oxfords, silk blouse and linen slacks were ruined. Or that she was in a luxury car with a man she hadn't laid eyes on until she ran into him.

What she cared about was Tori, and the horrible guilt that everything that had happened was all her fault because she'd been so distracted. If she hadn't been so worried about Tori understanding where she was coming from, and if she hadn't been so preoccupied with the answer on her bid on the contract, none of this would be happening.

An uncharacteristically quiet Tori was in the front seat while the driver made his way through the heavy rain and slick streets. And despite the fact that they had just been in an accident, Dylan had to grudgingly admit that the driver was good at controlling the car on the slick streets.

She sat forward, gripped the side of the passenger seat with one hand and leaned closer to ask Tori for the umpteenth time, "How are you?"

"Shh." Tori gently made circles on her large stomach with one hand, and held up her other hand to quiet Dylan. Then she sighed and seemingly sank back into the seat. "I'm fine. He just moved. It's okay."

Dylan spotted a car phone on the console and asked the driver, "Can I use your phone to call her husband?"

He never took his eyes off the road as he grabbed the phone, then held it back toward her. "Help yourself."

"I wish you wouldn't call Allan. He'll be worried sick," Tori said as Dylan pushed in Allan's work number.

"He has to know." Dylan hit the Send button with an annoyingly unsteady finger and said, "I'm so sorry. I could have killed both of you."

"Well, you didn't. Not that you didn't try."

"I know, I know," she muttered, then heard Allan's secretary answer the call. Quickly she told the woman what was going on and asked her to find Allan and send him over to the hospital as soon as possible. Once she was satisfied the woman would contact Allan right away, she hit End and offered the phone back to the driver. "Thanks so much."

"I told you to watch where you were going," Tori said in a low voice.

"I wish I had, but I had things on my mind. I should have let you get a cab, but I thought I could help, and it was raining."

Even when Dylan was trying to apologize and console her sister, Tori couldn't quite let things rest. "Your car looked pretty badly damaged, and with everything else that's happened, your insurance is going to go through the roof."

Her sister knew her weak points down to the last letter. Dylan had had a couple of tickets and a few small accidents in the past year and her insurance had already gone up once. But she couldn't think about that right now. She passed it off with "It might, but as long as you're okay, Tori, that's all that counts."

"And this nice man is taking us to the hospital so the doctor can tell you everything's just fine."

Nice man? Dylan glanced at the driver. For the first time since she'd looked up in horror to realize they were going to crash, she actually saw him clearly instead of through the rain with fear racing through her.

She'd realized even then that he was tall, well over six feet in height, and large, with broad shoulders and muscular arms exposed by the clinging dampness of his casual cotton-chambray shirt. Now she noticed his strong hands with square-tipped fingers gripping the leather steering wheel, and as she looked from his hands to his face, he turned and glanced over his shoulder at her.

His gaze was intense and direct, from eyes as dark as the night under a slash of straight eyebrows and framed by thick, short lashes. An instant connection with the stranger actually caused her breath to catch in her chest, and before she looked away to regroup, the man's image seemed to burn into her being.

His skin was tanned, his nose looked as if it might have been broken more than once in the past. Almost-shoulder-length sandy brown hair had been darkened by the rain and slicked back with a careless hand from a face dominated by roughly hewn features. There was a certain sensuality in the set of his lips and in the strength of his jawline. He was a man who demanded attention—a man she could only label "uncomfortably male."

"You're a Good Samaritan," Tori was saying to the man. "And I appreciate it. Even though I think it's totally unnecessary." Dylan didn't have to look at Tori to know her sister had cast her a dark glance before she said, "And now my husband's going to be going crazy."

The driver spoke for the first time since the three of them had gotten into the Mercedes, and the voice fit the man: deep and vaguely rough, a voice that filled all the spaces in the car even though it wasn't particularly loud at all. "I'm no Good Samaritan."

"Of course, you are. After all, Dylan's the one who hit you. It wasn't your fault, but you're taking your time to drive us to the hospital. And I appreciate it very much."

The driver glanced at Dylan again, and unexpectedly said, "Dylan?"

"My sister, Dylan Bradford. And I'm Victoria Pallum, but I'm called Tori."

"Cooper Reeves," he said as he looked back at the road ahead of them.

"Mr. Reeves—"

He interrupted Tori with, "Call me Coop, please." Then he pointed ahead of them. "Is that the hospital?"

Dylan glanced out the rain-streaked window and saw the soaring structure of Doctor's Memorial against the gray backdrop of the day. "That's it," she replied. "Go to Emergency, then take that turn on the right to the entrance."

He was doing what she said even as she was saying it, and pulled under a portico in the glow of the red Emergency sign beside a series of glass doors. Dylan scrambled out, but before she could close her door, Coop was by the passenger door, opening it for Tori. While he offered her his hand and eased her out, he spoke to Dylan. "Go and get someone to help get her inside."

She was taken aback by his tone of authority, but didn't hesitate in heading for the center doors. In a waiting room that was partially filled with people, she hurried over to the windows on the far side marked Check-in. A middle-aged nurse with hawkish features was sitting behind the open window and looked up at Dylan.

"Yes, ma'am?"

"My sister's outside, and we were in an accident. She's pregnant and—"

Before she could get anything else out, the nurse was on her feet. "Accident victim! Front doors!" she called behind her.

Double metal doors to the right opened almost immediately, and two green clad men rushed forward with a stretcher on wheels. They ran for the entry and were outside within seconds. When Dylan would have followed them, the nurse stopped her by saying, "I need you to give me information about the patient, about her insurance. We also need her doctor's name so we can contact him."

Dylan spoke to the nurse as she kept her eyes on the doors. She could see the attendants helping Tori onto the stretcher, then they were coming back inside with Coop right behind them.

They pushed the stretcher toward the metal doors, and Dylan moved quickly to follow them. But one of the men stopped her. "Stay out here, and we'll come and get you and her husband as soon as the doctor can check her."

She wanted to fight the order, to go with Tori. She hated the sight of her sister on the stretcher, her stomach looking enormous and her face tugged in a deep frown. But when she would have gone after them through the metal doors, a hand stopped her, holding her back. Then a voice was by her ear, saying, "Let them do their thing. Your sister's in good hands."

As she turned, she found Coop right beside her and suddenly the heat of his hand registered with her. At the same time she knew an irrational impulse to hold on to that hand and never let go. The inclination was totally foreign to her.

She'd always thought she was a strong person, a person who led and didn't follow, who took control and didn't weaken in a crisis. She hated the idea of women who swooned or fell apart, but right now she felt way out of her depth. And this stranger with dark, unreadable eyes was looking suspiciously like an anchor to her.

She pushed her hands behind her back and took a deep breath as his hold released her and she was truly on her own again. "I should be with her," she whispered, recognizing the flatness in her own voice.

"She knows you're out here. And they'll let you know as soon as they check her out."

Sensible words. Words that should have made her feel better, but words that only made her guilt grow. "God, I can't believe this happened." She moved away from Coop, needing distance between herself and the man, and also needing to move. She could feel him right beside her as she crossed to an area with windows that looked out into the dark gray world where the rain had settled into an annoying drizzle. The black Mercedes was still beside the curb, its polished surface glistening as security lights snapped on around the emergency entrance.

She frowned at the way the trunk of the luxury car was slightly sprung, and the way the even lines of the rear were definitely askew. She had a general idea of the price of those cars, and knew it would probably cost an arm and a leg to repair it. An arm and a leg that she didn't have and didn't want to charge to her insurance right now.

"I can't believe that I ran into the Mercedes like that," she murmured with a shake of her head.

"Are you from around here?" Coop asked from her right.

"I've lived here all my life."

"Then that's your problem."

She turned and Coop was less than a foot from her, but thankfully he was looking out at the black car. "What's my problem?"

Suddenly his dark eyes turned on her and the glare of the overhead light exposed the fact that their color was a deep, chocolate brown with a flaring of gold. "From what I hear, Californians aren't supposed to know how to drive in the rain," he said with a slight tilt at the corners of his mouth that only intensified the man's impact on her. "I've heard it never rains in California."

"Never believe what you hear."

He motioned with his head toward his car and the rainy early evening through the windows. "I learned that the hard way."

She could feel a touch of heat in her cheeks at his pointed comment. "I'm really sorry for what happened to your beautiful car, but if you hadn't stopped right in the middle of the lane without warning, I wouldn't have had the chance to hit your car at all. Would I?"

"Oh, I think you would have managed to do it, one way or the other," he murmured with a slight smile.

"Excuse me?"

"You barely missed me before you finally made contact."

"You were driving as if you were in a parking lot," she muttered. "And the rain..." Her words trailed off when Coop suddenly smiled—a devastating expression that crinkled the corners of his eyes and made her have the most ludicrous idea that the sun had just come out and banished the gray rain.

"I *was* in a parking lot."

"Okay , okay," she said, more than a bit flustered. "And I concede the fact that this whole thing was my fault. I didn't see you. I was preoccupied, and I'm sorry."

Thankfully his expression sobered at bit, leaving just a trace of a twinkle in the depths of his eyes as he murmured, "Mea culpa?"

The man was getting to her on so many levels, she couldn't even begin to fathom them all. So she wrote them off to the stress of the moment, and tried to ignore the way the man's closeness was making her heart pound and her thought process get muddled. "Absolutely." She hesitated, then said, "I know you're probably dying to go do whatever it was you were going to do when I hit you.''

"I'm not in any hurry," he said.

"You weren't going shopping or home or something?"

"Actually, I was killing time. I just didn't plan on doing it this way."

"I wanted to ask you something about the car,"

"What's that?"

"I want to fix it."

"Of course. Just give me the name of your insurance company and—''

She crossed her arms on her chest and shook her head. "No, I mean, I'll pay for it. I'd just rather it didn't go through my insurance." She glanced out at his car again, then back at Coop. "I know it's an expensive car."

"Your car isn't chopped liver," he replied.

"My car's ten years old, and hardly close to the Mercedes. I know the repairs might be really expensive, and I might have to make payments, but I'll pay whatever it costs to fix it."

He studied her for a moment, then exhaled. "Oh, I understand."

"Excuse me?"

"You've got a history of having accidents and tickets, and if this goes on your insurance, your premium is going to skyrocket."

It was a statement, not a question, and he was exactly right. "I wouldn't use the word *history*," she said quickly, hedging more than a bit. "But I've had a few tickets and a couple of fender benders."

"And why's that?"

She rubbed her hands nervously on her upper arms. "I get distracted, and I admit that maybe I don't pay enough attention sometimes."

"And what distracts you?"

She grimaced. "Buildings, mostly."

She could see the smile coming back. "What do they do, jump into the road in front of you or wave at you as you go past?"

She wished she could smile, too, but her face felt tight. "I check out buildings the way some people check out cars or scenery. It's a by-product of my work."

"Which is?"

"Architectural restoration."

"Which is?"

He wasn't making this easy at all. "Taking old buildings, run-down buildings mostly, buildings that are going to go under the wrecker's ball, and restoring them to their former glory. I see buildings, and I get distracted, either by what they used to be, or by what they are now or what they could be."

"So, you were thinking about some old buildings right before you hit me?"

"I was talking to Tori about my work, yes, and I take full responsibility for your...*our* problem. And I just want to pay for it myself, because . . . Well, you know why. We can keep it between the two of us, can't we?"

He shrugged, tugging the fabric of his damp shirt across his wide shoulders. "I actually don't have a problem with that."

She sighed with relief. "Great, then we—"

"But," he said, cutting her off. "The person who loaned me the car might not be so agreeable."

Her heart sank as fast as her hopes of making this as painless as possible. "It's not yours?"

He shook his head, his damp hair brushing the collar of his shirt with the motion. "Nope."

"You're borrowing it?"

He nodded. "While I'm in San Diego."

She sank back against the cool wall by the window and the chill from marble inlay penetrated her damp top. She shivered involuntarily and wrapped her arms more tightly around herself, then glanced up at Coop in front of her. "So, you aren't from around here?"

"No."

"Your friend who owns the car, do you think he might be open to negotiations?"

"He's not a friend. He's a business associate, and I can tell you from personal experience, he loves negotiations." Any hope in those words was shot down when he finished with, "Actually, his pleasure comes when he chews people up and spits them out after he wins."

Dylan closed her eyes for a moment to try and regroup. Her insurance would choke her. And right now, she had to save every penny. If she won the contract bid, the money wouldn't be there for a while, and she would have to quit her job. She couldn't do both, so her savings were all she would have for a while.

"I've got a proposition for you," Coop said softly.

She opened her eyes when the sound of his voice made her stomach clench. He hadn't moved, and his effect on her hadn't changed. She had to force herself to take two even breaths before speaking. "Excuse me?"

"You said you were born and raised around here?"

"Yes, but—"

"So, you know this city."

"Sure, of course."

"On the other hand, I know how to deal with Jeb Brokaw, the car's owner."

She frowned as she stood straight. "I don't see—"

"How's your schedule for the next day or two?" he asked abruptly.

But before she could ask why he wanted to know, she heard someone call out, "Dylan?"

She glanced past Coop and saw Dr. Barnette coming toward her through the busy waiting area. The tiny balding man was dressed in a white coat over what looked like golfing clothes in a shocking lime green and yellow.

As Dylan quickly moved past Coop to meet the doctor halfway, she accidentally bumped into Coop's shoulder and stumbled sideways. The next thing she knew, Coop had a hold on her, his hand closing around her upper arm, his heat filtering through the damp material of her blouse sleeve.

"Steady," he said softly near her ear, then Dr. Barnette was in front of her.

She had to swallow hard to be able to force out the words, and she was more than thankful for Coop still holding on to her as she asked, "Is...is Tori all right?"

He nodded while he rubbed his hands together as if to warm them. "Actually, she's just fine." The man seldom smiled, and right now his brow was knit in a frown. "She's resting right now, and I'll keep her in overnight just to be sure, but as far as I can tell, she's in top shape. And the little one's just fine, too. Strong heartbeat, moving all around, very active, so we aren't expecting any immediate appearance."

Dylan felt light-headed with relief. "Oh, that's terrific," she breathed. "That's good news."

He glanced at Coop, then past the two of them. "And where's Allan?"

"He's on his way."

"When he gets here, tell him she's in for the night."

"Thank you for coming so quickly," Dylan said.

"I was actually going to play golf, but the rain ruined those plans. I'm on my way home now, but I've left orders that if Tori has a good night, she can go home in the morning."

Dr. Barnette glanced at Coop who was so close, Dylan felt as if his body heat was pushing away all the chill from the damp clothes and from the fear she'd had until moments ago.

"I'm sorry," the doctor said. "I don't believe we've met."

Coop held out a hand to Dr. Barnette. "Cooper Reeves."

As the men shook hands, Dr. Barnette shocked Dylan when he said, "I knew when Tori got married and started a family, Dylan wouldn't be too far behind. Nice to meet you, Mr. Reeves."

Dylan darted a look at Coop, waiting for him to set the doctor right, but he merely nodded and said smoothly, "Dylan isn't too far behind anything these days."

Color burned her cheeks, but before she could interject some sanity, someone called her name again. "Dylan!" And this time Allan was there, running toward her, uncaring that he bumped into a couple of people in the process. Tall and lanky, he was out of breath when he stopped in front of her. His blond paleness was touched by high color and his short, light hair was damp from the rain.

"Where is she? What's wrong? You didn't tell my secretary more when you called."

"Everything's all right now," Dylan said as she reached out to touch his arm. "She's in her room, and she's going to stay for the night, but—"

He cut her off by turning to Dr. Barnette and asking, "Doc, what's going on?"

The doctor quietly took Allan by his upper arm and gently drew him back across the room. "I'll take you to Tori," he said. "And while we walk, we can talk."

Dylan stood where she was, watching Allan and Dr. Barnette head for the double metal doors by the reception window. When they disappeared behind the heavy barriers, Dylan felt completely cut off and alone.

"Aren't you going to see your sister, too?" Coop asked.

She wasn't alone. A stranger was still there, a stranger who had the oddest ability to make her feel as if he was supporting her without even touching her. She stared at the doors and knew she was a coward. She wasn't up to facing Tori just yet. "I—I think I should give Allan a few minutes with her first."

"Good idea."

As she closed her eyes for a moment to calm down, she felt Coop cup her elbow, his fingers strong and sure through the dampness of her blouse sleeve. As she took a breath and turned to glance up into his dark eyes, she didn't understand why the impulse to hold on to him was so very close to the surface all the time. Or where that need came from. But she didn't fight him when he urged her over to the chairs beside the windows.

Gratefully, she sank down on the plastic cushions, her legs precariously weak all of a sudden. Coop crouched down in front of her, lightly resting his hands on his thighs and squinting slightly as his dark eyes studied her.

"Hey, I don't know you very well—really not at all, but even I can see that you're beating yourself up over this whole thing."

Dylan had never been one to wallow in self-pity of any sort, but she was perilously close to doing that right now. "It's all my fault."

"Sure, it is," he said without hesitation, not hedging a little bit. "But there's an old saying about this very thing."

"What?"

"There are good accidents and bad accidents. The good ones are when everyone walks away in one piece. You walked and she walked. It's good. Believe me, very good. Despite the cars looking worse for the wear. Another old saying is, 'It's the people that count, not the cars,' and that's that."

She was shocked that she almost felt the tugging of a smile at the corners of her mouth. "You just made all that up, didn't you?"

"No, they're old, old sayings that work for me." As he spoke, he startled her by reaching out and touching her knee with the tips of his fingers. Not an intimate touch by any definition, but that didn't stop her breath from catching in her chest or making any traces of a smile falter. "'Timing is everything in life.' Another old saying that's very true," he said softly.

As his touch lingered on her knee, she knew that timing was the only thing that could account for this man with dark eyes coming into her life here and now. Accident or fate? She didn't take the time to think it through right then. "I've heard that saying," she replied, her voice slightly tight in her own ears.

"Then consider timing and everything that goes with it, and give yourself a break. Then, let's move on."

She wished she could just pass it all off that easily, but before she could object, Coop tapped her knee with the tips of his fingers. "Change of subject. Okay?"

She nodded.

"Good." He drew his hand back to rest it on his own thigh. "Now, I have a proposition for you."

Dylan had been vaguely relieved when he'd broken his contact with her, but any relief was long gone at the sound of his words—words that conjured up all sorts of images in her mind that didn't have a thing to do with cars or accidents or timing.

She'd been attracted to men, seeing someone who was sexy or interesting or intriguing. But she'd never met a man who was all of those things—and even more. And despite the fact that she was going to be thirty in eight months, she was at a loss trying to deal with this man and the way he could set things on their ears with a touch or a word.

She licked her lips, then finally managed to ask, "A...a proposition? What is it?"

And in that moment she literally held her breath, waiting for his answer.

Chapter Three

Coop was so close to Dylan he could see the flare of gray blue at the center of her irises. He knew if he took a deep breath he would catch her scent—the mingling of freshness and rain and a perfume that carried the light fragrance of blossoms.

He had to focus on his words and not on the woman in front of him if he hoped to make enough sense for her to agree to his offer. "After you see your sister and satisfy yourself that everything's going to be all right, do you have any plans for the next twenty-four hours or so?"

She stared at him for a long moment, then a fine line appeared between her eyes as she frowned. "Excuse me?"

"What are you planning to do for the next twenty-four hours?"

She shrugged. "Mostly work. Why?"

"At an office?"

"Not really. I'm doing something on my own."

"What's that?"

"I made a bid on a contract for restoration on buildings in the older section of the city, and I was going to look at them again to get some ideas. Then I'll go home and work on them."

Buildings? That wasn't what he'd had in mind to kill time, but if Dylan went with the tour, why not? "Can you take me with you to check them out?"

"Mr. Reeves, I don't—"

"Coop, it's Coop."

"What are you talking about?"

He moved back, rocking on his heels. "About my proposition. How would you feel about me talking to Brokaw and getting him to agree to have the car fixed without the insurance companies coming into it?"

She nodded immediately. "I'd really appreciate it."

"If I do that for you, would you do something for me?"

Her eyes widened, emphasizing their deep navy color. "What?"

"Show me around San Diego. Show me the city. Show me your buildings. Show me anything. I've got time and you know this city."

"You want me to be a tour guide?"

He'd never had a tour guide like her, but he wouldn't mind that one bit. "Sure. And things will work out for both of us."

"And you think you can get Mr. Brokaw to let me pay for the repairs?"

"I think I can get him to be agreeable about the arrangement. So, how about it?" When she hesitated in giving an answer, he realized how important it had become over the past few hours to make sure he didn't walk out of this place alone. Odd for a man who went through life alone, but right now, he didn't want to be alone at all. "I'd like to see your buildings," he heard himself saying, despite the fact that he had little if no interest in architecture. And it didn't stop him from adding, "They sound interesting."

That brought a sudden and brilliant smile to her face—an expression that made his heart almost skip a beat. "Sure, they do," she murmured dryly.

He shrugged, the damp fabric of his shirt tugging on his shoulders. "Hey, I'm open for anything, and if the buildings are fascinating to you, I'll give them a shot."

She held up her left hand and for the first time he noticed how slender her fingers were, how fine the bones were. "Enough. You don't have to make-believe buildings are anything more than buildings to you. There are very few people in this world who get a kick out of fascias and support beams."

He couldn't lie about a passion for buildings, so he completely ignored her statement. "Do we have a deal?"

Her hand slowly lowered to her blouse, skimming over the mussed silk on her high breasts and down to her wrinkled linen slacks. "I need to see Tori, and these clothes..." She brushed at the rumpled material several times. "I'm a terrible mess."

He wanted to say she looked infinitely lovely, with tendrils of hair clinging to her delicate skin, and her slender shoulders and arms defined by the damp material of her blouse. But he knew it would sound too much like a line, especially after his absurd reassurances about a desire to look at buildings.

So he slowly stood. "No problem. See your sister, go and change, and we'll take it from there." He looked down at her eyes where her lashes partially veiled her expression. "How about it?"

She exhaled on a soft sigh, then pushed up out of the chair to face him. "If you can get this Brokaw person to cooperate, I don't see why I couldn't show you around San Diego a bit." She brushed at a stray curl by her cheek. "Just let me know where you'll be, and if your friend agrees to the arrangement, then I can—"

He stopped that immediately. "Go in and see your sister, and meanwhile I'll run back to my hotel to change and contact Brokaw. Then I'll come back here and let you know what's happening."

"That's too much trouble."

He put his hands behind his back when she swiped at the stray curl again, just as ineffectively as before. The urge to smooth it for her was very real, just as real as his determination not to let this end with a phone call and tentative plans to see the city. "Just go and see your sister, and I'll be back."

She hesitated as if she couldn't quite figure out what to do, so he took the decision out of her hands.

"I'll be back in an hour."

"Okay, in an hour. I'll see you then," she murmured, then moved past him to the doors. He didn't turn to see her leave, but headed for the exit himself and went out into the night.

The steadily misting rain haloed the security lights at the side of the hospital, and the sky was completely black now. As he ducked his head and ran for the Mercedes, he had a niggling feeling that this situation wasn't like any other he'd been in before. He slipped inside the car and as he closed the door, he thought he caught the lingering scent of Dylan in the air.

An illusion, he assured himself with a shake of his head, but as close to being real as what felt like a need to see Dylan again—to talk to her, to get to know her, and to have her presence push back the emptiness of the city all around him.

As he raked his fingers through his rain-dampened hair, then started the car and drove off, that last, lingering thought about need wouldn't leave him. Since when had he needed anything or anyone—especially someone to fill voids in his life?

He'd never needed anyone before. He'd always walked away when he wanted to, living life by his rules, needing no one. He'd never liked ties or bonds nor let himself depend on anyone but himself.

Brokaw had told him he took everything to the limit, that he came to the edge of disaster time and time again without blinking, because he didn't have anything to lose. There was no one to answer to but his employer. And no one to grieve for him if he didn't make it out of a tight turn or if he didn't walk away from a crash.

If that was the way he was perceived, he didn't care. He liked his life. He liked what he did and how he did it. But that didn't stop him from admitting that what he wanted right now was to talk with Brokaw and get back here in an hour to see Dylan again.

IT WAS ALMOST SEVEN o'clock and completely dark outside when Dylan left Tori and Allan alone in Tori's room and stepped out into the green-tiled corridor on the seventh floor of the hospital.

There were a number of people—both staff and visitors—milling around in the hallway, but one glance told her there was no tall, sandy-haired man anywhere in sight. She'd thought about him being outside the door the whole time she'd been talking to Tori and Allan. When she'd stepped out of the room, she'd felt slightly nervous about the idea of seeing him again.

But he wasn't waiting, and she wasn't at all sure if she was relieved or disappointed. As she started down the corridor toward the bank of elevators, she admitted that it could be for the best that he hadn't come back and that everything might be settled with a phone call. The man was a distraction, and right now, that was the last thing she needed in her life.

As she stopped by the elevator doors and pushed the Down button, she took a deep breath. Today had been so crazy, the last thing she needed was to be around a man who only added to that craziness and emphasized her uncomfortable feeling that she was very close to losing control of everything . . . including herself.

With a ding, the elevator directional light lit up pointing down, then the doors slid open. As if her thoughts had conjured up the image, Coop was there, in the car, right in front of her. He'd changed into a cream-colored, band-collar, long-sleeved shirt and its soft material clung to the width of his shoulders. Dark brown slacks molded to strong legs and were worn with suede boots.

The idea that he was just as devastating as she remembered had barely materialized when her gaze met his dark eyes. The craziness of the day came back full force, embodied by this man. It didn't make sense, any more than it made sense that his sudden appearance made her decidedly light-headed and her legs felt as if they'd lost all ability to keep her standing.

She reached out for the support of the wall, but Coop was there, catching her by her shoulders. In a blur, she found herself leaning back against the coldness of the wall with all the heat in the world coming from Coop holding her by her shoulders, mingling with his breath brushing her skin as he leaned closer to her.

An anchor. The man had become her anchor, and that bothered her almost as much as her uncharacteristic weakness. He was literally holding her up, providing the strength to keep from sinking to the floor.

And he was saying something to her, but she didn't have a clue what it was until she concentrated on it.

"You're white as a sheet. Are you all right?" he asked, his voice rough with concern. "It's not your sister, is it? I thought that was settled, that she was—"

"No, no, it's not," she said in a breathless voice she barely recognized as her own. "Tori... She's doing fine." She resisted the urge to touch his chest. Instead, she pressed her palms flat against the wall at her side, the chill offsetting a heat that was insidiously invading her the longer he touched her. "It's just things...." As her voice trailed off, words failing her, she took a shaky breath.

He looked both ways in the corridor. "Damn it, it's a hospital, and there isn't a doctor in sight. What in the hell—"

"No, I—I don't need a doctor," she said quickly. A doctor wouldn't have any pill that would make this man less disturbing to her. "I just got a bit light-headed for a minute. That's all."

"You went as white as a sheet," he murmured, those dark eyes on her, full force, studying her. Then his hand shifted, but instead of breaking the contact, the tips of his fingers brushed her cheek, making her tremble. "God, you're cold. Are you going to faint?"

And he was hot. "I'll be fine." She wasn't at all sure about that as she took another breath. "I—I just need some fresh air." She cautiously pushed away from the wall. All she wanted was to have him let her go so she could breathe again without this tightness.

Thankfully he let her go and moved back, and her legs held her upright. "Are you sure you're not going to faint?" he asked, not sounding very convinced.

"I've never fainted," she muttered, keeping her eyes down as she brushed at her mussed blouse and felt her world start to settle.

"There's a first time for everything." He spoke so softly, she drew her head up to look at him. She regretted the action when he suddenly smiled, and the expression jolted through her—a first time for that sort of reaction to a simple smile. "But are you sure?" he asked.

"I'm sure." She turned quickly to face the elevator doors and block his image from her.

But that didn't stop him from finishing with "Do you think you can you walk on your own, or do you need some help?"

The idea of the alternative to her walking on her own came to her, and she could almost hate him for causing a barrage of fantasies with his question. Fantasies that had no place in a hospital, much less with a stranger; fantasies of being carried off into— She stopped that thought right there, closed her eyes tightly and took another breath. "I can do it myself," she said.

"Then let's get out of here," he replied, and she felt him brush her arm. When she opened her eyes, she saw that he'd pressed the Down button on the elevator panel.

The car came almost immediately, and Dylan moved quickly inside as soon as the doors opened. Then, as they started down, she hugged her arms around herself and turned to face the doors.

"So, your sister's really okay?" Coop asked, his voice muffled a bit in the interior of the elevator.

Much better than she was right now, she thought, staring hard at the lit floor numbers over the door. "She'll be fine."

"Good," he said softly.

Dylan looked down at her own reflection in the polished metal doors, and Coop's was right beside hers. A certain tangy freshness filtered through the air as she inhaled again, mingling with something she could only label as a certain maleness that seemed to cling to the man.

When she glanced at his face in the reflection and met his gaze, a lurching of her heart forced her to take a sharp breath. Quickly, she looked down at her hands clasped tightly in front of her and found herself grasping at rational thoughts and reactions. She hated that sense of being on the brink of losing control, and she hated the way her mouth went dry at just one glance from those dark eyes.

Fighting for the sanity she thought she'd started the day possessing, she tried to bring this encounter back to the footing it should have had. "Did...did you get to talk to your friend, Mr. Brokaw?"

"Yes, and it's all settled. He said he didn't care who paid, as long as it's taken care of. In fact, he'll pay for it, then send you the bill, and he'll take it in payments."

She exhaled with relief. Finally, something was going right. "That's great."

"He wasn't too worried about it," he said. "The man sees cars as disposable, actually. And he was more worried about someone getting hurt. But since everyone's in one piece and happy, he's fine with it."

She hardly saw a Mercedes as disposable, not any more than she could say Tori was happy right now. "My sister's in one piece, but she's far from happy." There was no way she would tell Coop that Tori was madder than a wet hen at having to stay in the hospital for the night and having her last chance for an evening with Allan wiped out. "She's not pleased being in a hospital," she said, pushing aside any thoughts of black nightgowns and last chances at sex.

"I know I hate them."

"Tori's not a good patient, and just being around her is hard since she got in this . . . condition, let alone being around her when she's confined to bed."

"She's not happy about having a child?"

"Oh, far from it. She's actually in love with being pregnant and having a child and being a mother." She was telling the truth now, and the words came easily to her. "She's born to be a mother."

The elevator stopped and when the doors slid open, Dylan stepped out into the busy corridor near the entry lobby. Without looking at Coop, she headed for the front doors, thankful to be able to finally take a breath without the scent of Coop filling it.

But she didn't get off completely. Even though they were in a crowded lobby, she could literally sense Coop falling into step right by her side. It was unsettling that she knew how close he was to her without actually seeing him or touching him.

"I've heard about women like that," he said, matching her stride. "Born mothers."

"Oh, that's Tori, all right," she murmured as she glanced through the glass doors ahead of them at the rain that had slowed to a misty drizzle. "Home, hearth and family. A perfect definition of my sister."

"And how about you?" Coop asked when the automatic doors opened as they approached them.

They stepped out together into the dampness of the night and the protection of the front portico. Dylan headed for the curb as she asked, "What *about* me?"

"Is hearth, home and family the perfect definition for you, too?"

She glanced to her right as she stopped by the curb and found it almost easy to smile at that question now that they were out of the tight confines of the elevator. "Me? Not even close."

His head tilted to one side and his eyes narrowed on her as he tucked the tips of his fingers into the pockets of his slacks. "How do *you* define yourself?"

She'd never thought of defining herself to anyone before. And she wasn't comfortable starting the process with this stranger. "Where did you park?" she asked, hoping to divert this conversation away from herself.

"Over there." He motioned beyond Dylan toward an area to the left marked Patient Pickup. "It was the closest I could get to the protection of the roof."

She turned toward the black car partially protected by the overhang, and as Coop went with her, she nervously tried to tuck a few loose tendrils back into the confines of the knot. As they approached the car, she saw the way the trunk was vaguely bowed and the strange angle of the back bumper at one side. "What a mess," she muttered. "Thank goodness your friend was so nice about it all when it looks like that."

Coop was right beside her and when he spoke, it felt as if he was close enough for her to feel his breath against her ear. "He never actually saw it. I told him about it over the phone and assured him I've seen a lot worse."

"Do you make a habit of viewing accidents and assessing damage?" she asked.

That brought a soft chuckle and she was drawn to it even though she didn't understand it. She looked at Coop, who had the suggestion of a smile on his lips, and she had to blink to try and get her bearings.

"It's part of my work—evaluating damages to cars—and I've seen my share of accidents." He motioned her toward the passenger side of the car. "Get in, and I'll take you to your place to change, then we can start our tour."

When he moved, she thought he was going to touch her, and she was certain she didn't want that to happen. Not again, not now—now when she was having real trouble keeping her world balanced. She moved quickly to one side, and felt foolish about her instant reaction when he reached past her to open the door for her.

Without looking at him, she scrambled inside and as she sank into the supple leather, she saw her purse sitting on the console between the seats. She'd completely forgotten about it when she'd gotten out earlier, when she'd been distracted by everything—Tori, the accident ... and Coop.

As she pulled it into her lap, Coop slipped in behind the wheel and started the car. If she'd thought it had been hard to breathe in the elevator, the car felt positively claustrophobic. Dylan looked away into the misty night and racked her brain to think of some inoffensive, believable way to get out of here as quickly and as cleanly as possible.

The rain and the night were all she could see in the arc of the headlights, and they were her answer. "I think I'll have to give you a rain check on your tour, no pun intended, but it's so dark and rainy right now. There's not much to see or do around here at night."

As Coop drove toward the exit of the parking lot, he spoke softly. "I've found that some of the most interesting things to do are done after dark."

Her hands on her purse tightened as he did it to her again, producing treacherous fantasies that exploded in her imagination with such impact that she barely contained a gasp. Yet when she dared to look back at him, he appeared unaware of what he'd just said. His attention seemed to be on getting to the exit of the lot. "Excuse me?" she managed to ask.

"You're excused," he murmured.

"No, I meant, what—"

He cut her off with, "Just trust me. I'm an expert on things to do at night." He never looked at her as he spoke. "I've had a lot of practice."

Damn it, she could barely breathe now. She didn't doubt he'd had a lot of practice at a lot of things, especially playing word games with a woman who until right now had never thought of herself as vulnerable to innuendo or sensual suggestions. And boy, this wasn't what she wanted. She wanted her sanity back, and she was almost certain that sanity and Cooper Reeves didn't even fit in the same sentence, let alone the same space in the world.

Before she could stop the words, she blurted out, "I don't think this is such a good idea."

"What isn't?" he asked.

"This... this..."

"You giving me a tour of San Diego?" he asked softly.

You driving me crazy, she wanted to say. *You speaking in that seductive way, no matter what the words being said.* But she settled for, "This whole day. It's been too crazy." An absolute truth. "And I'm..."

She reached for the right word, but didn't have a chance before he spoke again.

"You're what? An expert on San Diego, wearing damp clothes and worried sick about her sister?"

"That about covers it," she said with a deep sigh.

He glanced at her through the shadows. "Then let me take care of everything."

That was just what she didn't want—him taking care of her or taking care of things. "No," she replied with more brusqueness than she intended. "Tell you what, you can just drop me off at my house, then if the rain stops tomorrow, I could—"

"I thought a deal was a deal," he said as he stopped with a jerking abruptness just before the exit gate of the parking lot.

"Of course, it is, but it's raining and—"

His dark, slanting glance riveted her, cutting off her words. He didn't make any effort to drive out onto the street, but instead, he clasped the top of the steering wheel with both hands and spoke through the shadows to her. "Hey, I'm sorry. If you don't want to do this, forget it. I'm not going to force you to. I thought we could—" He cut off his own words with a harsh exhale of air. "Damn it, I'm going about this totally wrong."

She was holding on to her purse so tightly that her hands ached now. "Going about what?"

He looked away from her into the night, but didn't drive any farther. The motor idled while the rain fell, and the tension in the car was almost painful until he suddenly raked his fingers through his hair, then gripped the steering wheel again. He stared out through the rain-streaked windshield. "It's time for the truth," he finally said.

"Excuse me?"

"The truth," he repeated, then looked back at her, the shadows doing little to dilute the strength of his gaze on her. "The truth is, I have no place to go tonight, and I don't want to go back to some lousy hotel room, watch reruns of *Gilligan's Island* and be kept awake wondering why in the hell the Professor and Mary Ann never got together."

Dylan stared at him, not sure that she'd heard him right. "What?"

"They never did it, did they? I mean, I think I've seen every episode at one time or another, and they never got it on. Unless I missed it. And if I missed it, I'm mad."

She had no idea where the laughter came from, but it bubbled up in her and although she could feel hysteria tinging it a bit, she welcomed it. "Nobody did anything on that island."

"What about the Howells?"

"Well, they shared the same hut. I just assumed—"

"Since they were married, they were beyond all that physical stuff?"

"No, no," she said, chuckling at the thought of Tori making that mad dash for the black nightgown.

"Okay, enough of them," he said. "Please, save me that madness. We can drive in the rain, or get something to eat, or go on a tour of the drainage systems in the city. Anything but the crew and guests on the *Minnow*. You know, I know all of the words to that damned song?"

She exhaled and let her head rest back against the leather of the seat. The laughter was dying, but something in her had eased with it. Suddenly it seemed so simple. Just a few hours, killing time for him. And she knew that she really owed him after he'd gotten his friend to go so easy on her with the car.

"Well?" he asked. "Do you want me to sing the Gilligan theme for you?"

"No, it's okay. I'll do the tour." She let herself relax a bit, releasing her death grip on her purse. "We'll figure out something to do, something a bit more interesting than a tour of the drainage system."

He was silent for what seemed an eternity, then brought tension back with a jolt when he said softly, suggestively, "Oh, I know we can."

Chapter Four

Dylan pushed back nearer to the door and tension tightened her shoulders and neck. She hated the way Coop could shift gears so completely, pulling her along with him on an emotional roller coaster with just a few words. And she hated the laughter ending. Especially when it had been such an effective barrier against whatever was happening between herself and Coop.

"How do we get to your place?" Coop asked.

She quickly gave him directions and knew the best she could do was to get this over with. But it wasn't going to be that easy, she found out when he pulled out onto the street and spoke again. "So, how do you define yourself if it's not home, hearth and family?"

She looked away into the rainy night and murmured, "I don't know."

"Okay, let's make this easier on both of us."

"Excuse me?" she asked, shifting in the seat to press partially against the door so she could look at his dark profile.

"We've never been formally introduced, and I think we need to be, but since there's no one to do it, why don't we do it ourselves? I'll go first."

She was very aware of the way his hair was brushed back from his face, the strong line of his jaw and the light from the streetlights playing watery shadows over his face. This seemed to be a reasonably safe diversion and she quickly agreed. "Okay."

"Cooper Mason Reeves. Age, thirty-six. No brothers, no sisters. My home base is an apartment I keep in New York. But I'm seldom there. Favorite color is red. I don't have a clue what my sign is, but my birthday's May first. Size twelve shoes and I'm not overly fond of *Gilligan's Island.*"

This was much easier. "Why are you in San Diego?" she asked.

"Waiting to find out if I have a job for the next five years, and the decision's due in the next day or two."

"Just what do you do?"

"I do prototype work with cars."

"What's that?"

'New models, new ideas. Testing them out to make sure they do what they're supposed to do."

"Like engineering?"

"No, more like track testing."

"You mean on racetracks, and running into walls to see what happens? I thought they used dummies for that."

He chuckled softly. "Some people might think they are using dummies. But we don't *try* to run into walls—just try to get around racetracks and maneuver tight curves."

"What about accidents?"

"Not if I'm lucky."

She could see how ludicrous it must be to him to have had a fender bender in a mall parking lot in San Diego after what he did for a living. "Just how lucky are you?" she asked.

He cast her a dark look as they neared the freeway-on ramp. "So far, so good."

"Except when you get hit from the back?"

"Sure, but that wasn't all bad," he said. "I'm not going to be watching reruns tonight. That's good. And no one was hurt. That's even better."

"You're been hurt before?"

"A few broken bones, bruises, cuts, abrasions. But the safety equipment on the cars is state-of-the-art. And you know the old saying: Any accident you walk away from is a—"

"Good accident," she finished for him.

"So far, so good."

She couldn't begin to figure out why the idea of Coop putting himself in life-and-death situations for money, or for the rush, or for whatever reason, made her feel slightly nauseated. "Aren't you ever afraid that the next accident might not be a *good* accident?"

"No. If I let myself be afraid, I wouldn't be any good to anyone in the business, least of all myself. Being afraid makes you hesitate when you shouldn't and pull back when you need to push it to the limit."

"So, you don't have any fear of what could happen?"

"Fear? Oh, hell, I've got that in spades. But there's a difference between fear and being afraid. Real fear is when you know you're taking the car to its limit and don't know if it's going to make it or tear apart. It's clean and sharp and vital. Brokaw says fear for me is like drugs to a junkie. I live for that moment of facing it and beating it." He laughed—a short, rough sound. "Brokaw's like your sister. He's always got an opinion."

"Is he right?"

"Probably more than I'd like to admit. He says that's why I like being alone, so there's no one who depends on me. That I can do what I want and not worry about anyone but myself. He should have been a therapist," he muttered, then abruptly switched the subject as he took the on-ramp. "Now it's your turn. Tell me about yourself?"

She looked away from him to the flashing lights of the oncoming cars on the freeway. An unrelieved tightness in her chest had crept up on her, a product of all the talk about fear and being afraid and being alone so he could take all the risks he wanted to take. She had truly never met another man like Cooper Reeves.

She took a breath. "Dylan Briar Bradford."

"Were you named after the eighteenth century Irish poet?"

She was surprised that he made that connection and looked back at him. "I think you're the first person who's ever asked about Dylan Briar. People usually think I was named after Bob Dylan, the singer. How did you hear about him?''

"One night when I was very drunk. I was with another driver, Tilly something or other, and he quoted the poet, something about how few men know when they've found their center—that perfect moment in their lives."

"*Portals of Time.* My father read that to me all the time and used to say that Briar was wrong, that most people knew about that perfect moment, but not until long after it happened. When it was too late to enjoy it."

"Maybe the poet was saying that life all boils down to living for the moment, and not for the past or the future. Then you don't have to worry about recognizing that single moment. You'll be living it."

Dylan could almost feel an edge in Coop, a part of him that believed exactly what he said. The part that pushed life to the limits and didn't look back. "Is that your philosophy for life?" she asked of him. "Live for the moment?"

"I'd say so," he murmured as he cast her a slanting glance. His expression was shadowed and protected by the night, but there was no protection for her from his voice that seemed to surround her when he spoke again. "Now, the question is, do you believe in living for the moment?"

Another question from Coop that made her stop in her tracks and back up, trying to figure out just what the answer was for it. "If you mean living and doing what you have to do, of course I do. But if you mean throwing everything off and just going for it, I don't think that's very smart."

"Smart? Does it have to be?"

"Maybe *smart* was the wrong word. Maybe it should be...*effective.* I mean, you have to plan for your future."

"Haven't you ever heard the old saying that life is what happens to you while you worry about what to do for your future?"

"Words," she muttered.

"True," he countered, and she could feel his gaze brush her as he glanced toward her, then back at the road. "You know what I think?"

She knew he would tell her, no matter what, but she asked, "No, what do you think?"

"That you just might need lessons in how to live for the moment."

"I'm doing just fine," she managed in a tight voice. "And I've been out of school for a long time."

"Maybe you need a graduate course."

She restored her death grip on her purse and looked away from Coop to the night flashing past. "I don't need anything but to get out of these clothes and—" She bit off her words as soon as she realized what she was saying.

But she wasn't fast enough. "Now, I'd say that's living for the moment."

Damn him. His words tipped her world totally out of balance and a heat that had little to do with the mechanical heater in the luxury car started to simmer in her. She closed her eyes tightly as she countered, "You know what I meant. They're damp and itchy."

"Of course."

Even when he agreed, she knew he didn't. "This is going to be a tour, not a philosophy lesson," she said with what firmness she could muster.

"Don't you think life is a philosophy lesson of sorts?"

She wasn't up to this at all. As she opened her eyes, she prompted, "Another old saying?"

"Just a thought. The way the idea of lessons was just a suggestion."

She caught movement and realized Coop was a blurred reflection in the side window. A dark man set against a dark night with only the illumination of the passing cars to shed light on him. "There's another old saying."

"Oh, what's that?"

"A tour guide gives tours, and a tourist isn't a student of philosophy."

"Does one rule out the other?"

"Actually, yes. I—I think we should concentrate on one thing at a time."

"I agree with that for now," Coop replied with annoying ease. "Right now, let's concentrate on you. We never got past your name."

Safe ground for now, she thought as she looked away from Coop into the rainy night outside. It was safer looking at the city than at the way the low glow from the instrument lights on the dash cast deep shadows on his cheekbones and throat, making him seem mysterious and perversely fascinating at the same time.

She cleared her throat, then began, "I'm twenty-nine years old, and only have the one sister, Tori. Our parents live in Florida in a condo complex that apparently has bridge games around the clock and cable television with a thousand stations. They're very content there. I have an admittedly spotted driving record, and I've lived in San Diego all my life."

"Birth date?"

"July fourth."

"Oh, so that's why they have fireworks?"

His gentle teasing was very welcome to her, easing her tension just a bit. "When I was little, that's what my dad used to say. 'Just for you, Dylan, just for your birthday,' and I believed him."

"What do you believe in now if it's not in home, hearth and family?"

She watched the way the city lights turned liquid and shimmering in the rain. "I didn't say I didn't believe in any of that. I've got a home, a restored adobe near Old Town, and it has a real fireplace, which definitely qualifies as a hearth."

"How about the family part?"

"I've got Tori and my parents."

"A husband?"

"No."

"Any little Dylans running around?"

"Absolutely not," she said quickly, and that brought a burst of laughter from him that took her a little off guard. "What's so funny?" she asked.

"The way you said that. Actually, I think I already know something about you."

"What's that?"

"You're not a born mother. In fact, I'd say you probably feel as if kids are like aliens. They're little people that you can't relate to. Little beings who scream and cry and spit up and generally disrupt life. Does that about cover it?"

She stared at him. "I don't know if I'd put it that way, but—"

"What did I leave out?"

She chuckled softly. "Okay, you just about said it all, but you sound as if you know about that, first-hand."

"I've thought the same thing myself from time to time." He exhaled, then took her totally by surprise when he added, "I guess, if I was completely honest, that was probably one of the main problems in my marriage."

Marriage? The word shocked her, and what shocked her even more was the fact that she hadn't even thought he might be married. And that was stupid. The man was attractive. The idea that there hadn't been other women to feel that way was more than stupid.

"You're married?"

"And divorced. It broke up a long time ago. You know that old saying about opposites attracting? Well, they might attract, but they don't last. I didn't want kids at all, and she knew it, but for some reason, she changed her mind and thought she could change mine.

"There's no way I'd bring a kid, even if I wanted one, which I don't, into my life when everything's so uncertain. She refused to understand that, or really couldn't. So that was it."

"I'm sorry," she said automatically, ignoring how relieved she was that he wasn't married now.

"Don't be. It was a long time ago, and probably a mistake from the start. It just took me a while to figure out my work was more important to me than just about anything else."

"You love what you do that much?"

He was quiet for a long moment, then said, "It's never boring. It fascinates me, and you can live for the moment without any apologies. I get a rush when everything goes right and comes together, and I'm damn good at it." He chuckled with a low, wry sound. "It's what I want to do. How about you? What do you want?"

"I want to get a positive answer on the bid I put in so I can start my own restoration business and probably work twenty-five-hour days for the rest of my life doing what I love to do." She shrugged. "Despite what

Tori thinks, I'm fine with that.'' She looked out the window and motioned ahead of them. ''Take the next off-ramp and go east.''

''I take it Tori doesn't believe you?'' he asked as he followed her directions.

''No matter how much I assure her it's the truth, she thinks— Well, she's opinionated.'' Dylan pointed ahead of them. ''Turn right on the next street, and my house is the last one on the left before the dead end.''

He followed her directions and soon they were approaching her house with rain misting through the ancient eucalyptus and oaks lining the way, and old-style streetlights casting a yellow halo in the night. Then she saw her house in the shadows with its thick adobe walls, wood trim and gated courtyard. It had been completely restored, and was one of the first jobs Dylan had ever done on her own.

When Coop parked the Mercedes on her ribbon driveway, she got out of the car and hurried around to the wrought-iron gate of the courtyard. Quickly, she pushed it back and went past the old olive tree in the center of the quarry-tile area to the shelter of the overhang at the entry. She unlocked the wooden door, but before she could push it open, Coop stopped her with a hand on her shoulder.

The touch was light but compelling, and as she slowly turned to her right to look up at him through the shadows, his hand shifted to keep the contact.

His voice was so low she had to concentrate to hear his words. "It's not that Tori is opinionated. I think it's that she can't figure you out, isn't it?"

Her tongue darted out to touch her lips. "No, not many people can."

His hold on her shifted again, trailing along the side of her throat to gently cup her chin. And she couldn't control a slight trembling from his touch, or hide from the fact that when he glanced at her lips, she knew she had wanted him to kiss her for what seemed forever.

"No, they can't," he whispered softly. "But I think I can."

"You can?"

"It all boils down to passion, doesn't it?" he breathed in a voice edged with roughness.

Passion? A single word brought back the fire—a fire fanned by his touch and his closeness on a dark, rainy night. The closeness of a stranger who made her imagine all sorts of things that were wild and insane and startlingly inviting at that moment.

"What...what does that mean?" she asked in a breathless whisper.

Coop was motionless, the touch of his hand on her feathery light while his gaze rested on her lips. But instead of leaning toward her, he murmured, "Passion. Full involvement in what you want. And your passions aren't hers. You like what you do. You focus on what you do, and I just bet you do a hell of job doing it."

She touched her lips with her tongue, almost regretting that there was no taste of him there. Then his hand left her, slowly letting her go, and she turned from him under the guise of opening the door. "How would you know that?" she asked.

"Because I'm the same way," he said from behind her, following her into her house as she went forward and reached for the light switch. "I get fully involved in what I'm doing. I never do anything I don't want to do, and my life is mine, but it's not what most people would choose."

"But you chose it?" she prompted as light flooded the living room that ran the width of the house at the front.

"It sort of chose me," he replied as she glanced back to him and found him studying the room, his dark eyes skimming over the space around them.

In the shadows of the car, she'd been able to minimize his image, shading it with softness and blurred detail. But now that he was in front of her and every feature was so distinct, she found herself squinting slightly to try and control her reactions to him.

She watched him take in the off-white walls of textured plaster and the polished wood-plank floors she'd restored to what they had been when the house had been built eighty years ago. If she'd had the money, she would have filled the room with antiques from that time, but right now she only had a scattering of throw rugs, a couch and chair by the fireplace, and a glass-topped table to the right of the door as a semblance of a dining area.

She had plenty of plants to fill in the gaps in decor, and she'd affixed to the walls prints from work that she'd done in the past. Her prize was an original rendering of the Santa Clare buildings by Winston Lee, the man who designed them for the city right after World War I.

"Home and hearth," Coop murmured as he crossed to the fireplace. He touched the top of the arch and brushed the tips of his fingers over the rough stone. Dylan barely covered a tremor that shook her when for that split second she remembered his touch outside the front door just moments ago.

She shook her head sharply and refocused as Coop drew back his hand and moved to one side to look at the black-and-white prints on the walls—before-and-after examples of her work; prints that she had been collecting for the day she had her own business and they could be displayed to impress prospective clients.

Now Coop studied them intently as he moved silently from picture to picture, until he was back to where she stood by the door. Then he glanced at the larger print of the Santa Clare buildings. "My buildings," she said. "That's the original drawing from the architect, Winston Lee. Circa 1919."

"So, I was right," he said as he turned to her with no more than a foot of space between them.

"About what?" she asked.

"Passion. It's in this house, in this room, in every print on the wall." He came even closer, with his deep and silky voice and the heat that seemed to emanate from him. There were no more buffers between them as he looked down into her eyes and whispered roughly, "And it's in you."

She wanted to say he didn't really know her. That he didn't have a clue about what she was or who she was. Or if there was passion there. But that would have been a lie. She had only known him for a few hours, but he'd told her more truths than she'd ever heard from family or friends. And she knew that what he was saying now was more than true.

He touched her cheek with one finger. The contact tentative, yet as strong as bands of steel, and she was incapable of moving away from it. Her breathing was all but nonexistent, and when he leaned toward her, she didn't move. Not even when his lips found hers.

Chapter Five

Coop knew the moment he felt the softness of her lips under his that he'd wanted to do this from his first glimpse of her in the rain. This wasn't mad impulse—something that he'd done on the spur of the moment. It had been a deep-seated need that was rocking him with its intensity. Yet the only contact was with her lips. He wasn't holding her or pulling her against him; he was just tasting her lips. But her essence engulfed him, surrounded him. And he was all but overwhelmed by a desire that licked like flames through his blood.

Nothing in his life had prepared him for this type of response from himself. Nothing had prepared him for the reality of Dylan Bradford. Or for a very unfamiliar twinge of uncertainty when she didn't respond. Slowly, he drew back just far enough to look into her navy blue eyes, more than aware of her softly parted lips and the sweetness of her breath with each rapid breath she took.

Her eyes were veiled by partially lowered lids, unreadable, and for a split second he was certain she was going to tell him to leave, to get out and keep going. He didn't have a clue what he would do if she did that, or worse yet, if she demanded an explanation for what he'd just done. What could he say? "I've wanted to kiss you from the first," or "The last thing I need is a tour guide"?

Instead, he found himself saying something flip and shallow. "Lesson one, living for the moment." The words were at odds with his feelings, which were anything but shallow and flip. He could feel their depth and strength, and he hated what he'd just said. The truth was he wasn't at all sure what else he could have said. He was at a loss with her in a way he'd never been with any other woman, and that was underscored by his instant reaction when her tongue gently touched her lips, as if tasting his kiss.

The simple action tightened his body even more and he pushed his hands behind his back and clenched them into fists. "Maybe I should just apologize," he said. "After all, you're the tour guide and—" He was babbling like some teenager in the throes of lust, and he hated it.

She shook her head abruptly, loosening her hair even more from its confines. And the idea of seeing it fall around her shoulders ran fire through him. "I...I need to change," she said quickly in an unsteady whisper, then quietly moved away from him.

He closed his eyes for a long moment as he listened to her footsteps on the wooden floor. Then her voice came to him again, but from a distance. "I'll be back in a few minutes," she said and was gone, leaving him alone.

"Take your time," he murmured to the empty room as he opened his eyes and saw a clock near the fireplace. It was only nine o'clock. He'd met Dylan five hours ago. Five hours, yet on some level it felt as if he'd known her all of his life.

For a brief moment he thought about the accidents he'd had. When time had stood still, when seconds had felt like hours, with life passing in slow motion while he waited for the inevitable impact. When time seemed to freeze. Instead these past five hours had felt like a mere blip in time, a flashing second of life, and yet he had the feeling that he could have lived a lifetime in five short hours.

DYLAN STOOD IN THE shadows of her bedroom at the rear of the house, the only light coming from the bathroom off to one side and the only sound, the slight patter of rain on the multipaned French doors that overlooked the back terrace.

It had taken her fifteen minutes to clean up and change into fresh clothes—a white pullover sweater and pleated navy slacks with casual leather boots. And those fifteen minutes helped her figure out what had happened with Coop.

Overreaction. She was stressed out waiting for word on the contract bid. Overreaction because of the accident and worrying about Tori. Overreaction because Coop was a man who seemed to exude sexuality. But the bottom line was that she was a tour guide.

"A tour guide," she whispered to herself as if saying it out loud could reinforce the fact. That was just what she was right then, despite the lingering sensations of the kiss that refused to dissipate, or thoughts of living for the moment.

She didn't want to get involved. She couldn't afford to get involved right now. She couldn't. She wouldn't. And the reason came to her so clearly that it rocked her. Cooper Reeves wouldn't be a simple involvement, if there was such a thing in this world. Cooper Reeves was a man who she knew without any proof could change her life forever if she let him. And she didn't want that to happen.

Before she realized what she was doing, she touched her tongue to her lips to taste him there. But that was as foolish as thinking she could be around a man like Coop and keep her distance. She scrubbed her hand over her mouth, took a deep breath and said firmly, "Tour guide." Then she opened the door and stepped out into the dark hallway, with every intention of making this tour thing as short as possible.

She took her time walking toward the glow from the front rooms at the end of the corridor, taking several deep breaths on the way. No more talk about passion, she told herself as she stepped into the living room.

She felt in control now. She had everything settled, a strong grip on sanity. Then she saw Coop on the couch, leaning forward, his elbows resting on his knees, and his head bowed.

Every rationale escaped her at that moment as she felt an aching need to go to him and touch him, to stroke his hair and feel it between her fingers. Protectively, she started to back up and regroup, but before she could do more than take a single step, he looked up as if he sensed her there. Slowly he stood and smiled slightly as his gaze flicked over her. "Ah, my tour guide returns."

In his words and stance, there was no trace of what had happened between them—not until she looked directly into his eyes. Even from across the room, she could feel the impact of that connection. And she knew she couldn't just pretend the kiss had never happened.

If she really believed she could go with him and keep her distance while she made good on her part of the deal, she wouldn't have said a thing. But she knew she couldn't. And she finally found the part of herself that never hedged or evaded that had been lost in the confusion of the past few hours. She usually faced things head-on, and this time wasn't going to be any different.

So she stayed where she was and forced out words that made her throat feel tight and uncomfortable: "You said you owed me an apology."

He didn't move, but she could tell he hadn't expected her to say anything. "I did," he replied evenly. "And I do."

"Thank you," she said.

He squinted slightly as he cocked his head to one side. "Do you want me to write that in blood?"

She could feel her stomach tightening with each word uttered, and she knew she should have let it go. She never should have mentioned it. But it was too late now. "No, I just wanted to make sure we understood each other."

Without warning, he breached her safety buffer by coming toward her and stopping so close to her that she had the odd impression she could feel him draw in each breath he took. He studied her intently, his eyes partially veiled by his lashes, then he slowly nodded. "Oh, I think we understand each other."

It was a new sensation for her to feel flustered and she hated it. Yet just his look, the way he stood so close and the essence of the man that came with each breath she took, did infinitely more than fluster her. When he reached out and touched her cheek with one finger, her thoughts went into a tailspin.

He glanced down at her lips again, and she could almost feel the caress before his gaze met hers again. "Don't we?"

"You... I..." she stammered as his finger followed the recent path of his gaze and rested like a feather on her bottom lip.

"Shh. Let's just leave it that we'll go with the flow." He smiled, with a crooked unsteady expression that belied his controlled exterior. "Live for the moment?"

The man made that sound so desirable, almost sane.

He slowly caressed her bottom lip as he spoke in a low, rough voice. "I think we both understand that I'm here for a day or two, tops. Then I'm out of here. We understand that you're waiting for an answer on your bid. Then, for all practical purposes, you're out of here, too. I'm killing time. You're killing time. And if we can do that together, I say that's great."

She almost felt hypnotized—a sensation that lasted until he broke their contact. Only then could she focus and make a vaguely coherent statement. "We... can see the city."

"That sounds like a plan." He exhaled. "So, where are we going?"

"Wherever you want to go."

He shrugged, a motion that tested the fabric of his shirt at his shoulders. "Food. I'm starving. How about you?"

Food had been the last thing on her mind, but now that he mentioned it, she was hungry. And a busy restaurant would be a very good buffer for them, with people all around. Then this feeling of intimacy that had been building so precariously between them from the first—and was overwhelming her—might be stopped. "Yes, I am hungry."

"Let's find a good restaurant and eat."

She nodded, then crossed to the door to pick up her purse where she'd left it on a side table. As she put it over her shoulder, Coop came over behind her and flipped off the overhead lights. For a moment they were standing in the dark, with the soft whisper of the rain on the window, and tension so palpable that Dylan was certain she could reach out and touch it.

Then Coop opened the door and the night invaded the house—the chill of the rain, the splashing of water running off the gutters, and the distant sound of traffic. Dylan quickly stepped out, took deep breaths of the cool air, and without looking at Coop, hurried toward the Mercedes.

THE RAIN STOPPED at eleven o'clock, the same time Dylan and Coop stepped out of a restaurant in the hills that overlooked the city and Harbor Bay. The night was increasingly chilly and a slight breeze skimming off the water played with the leaves of the trees and plants on the landscaped grounds of the Mexican restaurant.

As they walked to the parking lot in silence, Dylan was relieved that things had shifted into a safe area. The restaurant had been packed and noisy, and they'd spent dinner with Coop asking her questions about San Diego. She'd sounded like a tour guide, talking about the missions and history, and telling him about some of her favorite places around the city.

As they approached the Mercedes, Dylan glanced up at the night sky, at heavy clouds that rolled across the heavens, breaking up just enough to expose an almost-full moon. It was as if the kiss had never happened, and that gave her a bit of space to breathe easier. The night was almost over and she would make it, she thought, as she reached for the car door and opened it to slip into the leather interior.

But she was wrong—one more mistake in a day that had been filled with mistakes, starting with the accident. Although Coop settled behind the wheel and started the engine, he didn't drive off as if to take her home. Instead, he sat there with the engine idling and asked, "Now, where are those buildings of yours?"

She moved closer to the car door and turned slightly to look at him. The moonlight was beginning to invade the night and touched Coop, etching deep shadows at his throat and hiding his eyes. "The other side of Old Town, closer to the water."

"Just tell me where to go," he said.

She looked at the dash clock, then back at Coop. "But it's eleven o'clock."

"Oh, no," he said with a touch of humor in his voice. "Don't tell me you're a morning person, one of those disgustingly cheerful people at six in the morning who tend to collapse after eight at night?"

She found a smile for that. "Good grief, no. I'm not a morning person at all."

He let out an exaggerated sigh. "Thank goodness. Then we're in good shape for another couple of hours."

"A couple of hours?"

"Time enough to see your buildings."

"I don't have to point out that it's night and it's dark and no one's going to be there, do I?"

"How about lights? Is there any lighting there?"

"There are security lights, but—"

"Can we get inside?"

"I've got a key they gave me when I was studying it for the bid."

"Then there's no problem. I've heard enough about these buildings, and seen the original sketches, now I'd like to look for myself and see what all the fuss is about."

"You aren't serious, are you?"

"Absolutely. Do your duty as a tour guide and show me the buildings."

Just when she started to relax around Coop, he did something that brought everything back with a rush. Oddly, there was a part of her that actually wanted to show him the buildings, to share that with him, even though he was obviously just thinking up ways to keep busy.

"You're sure?"

"Definitely sure. I'd like to see them, to find out why they're so important to you," he said. "You know the old saying?"

"No, what old saying?"

"Never look a gift horse in the mouth."

She felt nervous laughter tickling in her. "I hardly think that fits."

"Then how about, I might not have another chance to ever see them, so it's here and now. This is it. What do you say?"

"Okay, okay," she said. "You win." Then she gave him directions and sat back.

As they drove through the city, the moon rose higher in the sky. She leaned against the passenger door with her shoulder and felt herself beginning to relax a bit.

Until he spoke again. "Live for the moment. Lesson number two," he said in a half whisper, then sped up as they drove off into the night.

COOP KNEW HE SHOULDN'T have given in to the temptation as soon as he'd said the words. He heard Dylan gasp softly, but she didn't say a thing.

For blocks and blocks she just sat there, and when he finally chanced a look in her direction, he could see she was staring out the side window, her hands clasped in her lap.

God, she looked so vulnerable and inviting, even in the blur of shadows. He gripped the steering wheel more tightly and wished he could read her mind, but he wasn't gifted that way at all. He had no idea if she was angry or bored or just ignoring him, and he wanted back some of that easy togetherness that had developed at the restaurant.

"Where to now?" he asked, even though his guess was they were just a few blocks from where those buildings of hers were located.

The wide street was lined with upscale restaurants, stores and a few small businesses. The facades looked as if they came from the past, like something around the turn of the century, with wired gaslights. And there were cobbled spots in the road. People were walking on the still-wet street, window-shopping, going into the restaurants and lining up at a theater offering a foreign film festival.

He turned to the right at the corner, heading toward the harbor, and immediately left behind all vestiges of pleasant, upscale city streets.

This road, with cracked blacktop, was darker, with half of the streetlights not working. There were no people on foot anywhere in sight, and no other cars. He could tell the area had slipped out of the main stream a long time ago.

Most of the multistory buildings were boarded up, and vandals had been active with graffiti. Despite the rain that had fallen most of the evening, the area didn't look at all clean, and Coop almost regretted saying he would come down here. But when he heard Dylan sigh softly by his side, and he glanced at her, he didn't regret it at all. Not any more than he regretted kissing her earlier.

"There's the main building," she said as she motioned ahead of them. "On the right, the one with the lights on by the doors, near the end of the street."

He glanced ahead at a grouping of buildings that were taller than the rest, one of them maybe twelve or thirteen stories high. "The famous buildings," he said as he slowed.

"The soon-to-be famous buildings," she replied. "*If* I get the contract."

He grimaced at the signs of disrepair and decay. "Did they ever think of a wrecking ball?"

"Oh, sure, that's the most-used solution for areas like this," she said, "but not the smartest."

He would have argued about that, but just said, "Really?"

"If they tore it down they'd lose so much. Just wait until you see inside. Winston Lee was so far ahead of his time in his use of space and his sense of spacial flow. If I do it, walls are going to come out, and some of the smaller sections will be absorbed, but the basic structure use is absolutely remarkable."

"I'm impressed," he said, and he was. But not with the building. He was impressed with her imagination that could find beauty in the midst of decay and neglect—one more of the special things he was learning about Dylan with each passing moment.

"Just wait until it's done. This street will make the one we were just on look run-down. It's going to be so fantastic, especially if we can get permits to redo the concrete areas with brick and—"

He slowed by the cluster of buildings. "You've got a great imagination."

"I've been told I have, although I'm not sure if I can imagine where you can park the car that's safe."

"Where do you park when you come down here?"

"I come during the day and I park right in front of the doors. Then I run."

"If that's good enough for you, it's good enough for me." He pulled into the curb right in front of the largest of the buildings, then glanced up and down the street. "You were going to come down here by yourself?"

"Until I got the job of tour guide," she replied as she opened her door. She was out before he knew it, and he hurried to get out himself. He went around the car and got to her side as she reached the entrance to the building.

He looked at her in the dull glow of the streetlight as she fiddled with a ring of keys. "Living dangerously?" he murmured.

She hesitated, then shrugged. "My sister says I do, but her idea of 'dangerous' is quitting one job before I have another. Nothing like the risks you take, that's for sure."

An incongruity registered with him then—something as incompatible as him standing on a street like this with a woman whose beauty could take his breath away. There was music echoing off the damaged walls of the closed buildings. Elvis Presley was singing "Blue Suede Shoes."

"Do you hear that?" he asked as he looked up and down the deserted street. "That's Elvis."

"He's been seen at a series of gas stations in Texas, too," she said as she put a key in the old lock and turned it.

"No, I mean, you can hear him singing?"

"It's coming from a place just around the corner near the water, a fifties club that just went in. The building used to be a gas station and garage, but they renovated it and now it looks like a dust-bowl warehouse. It's really popular." She shrugged. "They were going to make the whole place a parking lot, just tear it down and pave it over, but they were persuaded to rethink their position."

"Did you have anything to do with it?"

"A small part," she said as she unlocked the door and pushed it open with a protesting squeak. "The firm I work for did it—Barnes and Blazer. My contribution was finding pictures in the archives that convinced the city that they couldn't demolish fifties pop art."

He followed her inside, into an area that had a musty smell of age and neglect hanging in the stagnant air. A single overhead light cast a dull yellow glow over what appeared to be a reception area with high, shadowy ceilings and threadbare carpeting partially hidden by the clutter of boxes and pieces of furniture that had been stacked haphazardly.

The door clicked shut behind them, then Dylan led the way through the maze toward the back of the space. She kept up a running commentary about the building all the way, and he knew she was talking about its history and what she thought should be done to keep any restoration faithful to the original state.

But Coop lost track of the words as her voice softly echoed in the spaces around him. The light scent that seemed to cling to her brought freshness to the air that stirred about them. And he got another glimpse of the passion in her. She loved this. She was excited by it, and even though he didn't know a thing about what she was planning to do, that excitement and passion touched him.

When she stumbled slightly getting around metal filing cabinets stacked beside a huge wooden desk that formed a half circle in the middle of the space, she lurched toward him.

He felt her strike his arm, then his hand went out and he caught her around the shoulders, steadying her against his side. And the feeling of her in the circle of his arms blotted out everything around them.

Heat and softness, her quick breathing, her whispered, "I-I'm sorry," was all around him. Then she was looking up at him.

There was nothing else in his world right then but Dylan and holding her and wanting to kiss her again. Navy eyes, slightly parted lips, the sensation that he could almost feel her heart racing against him. And for that moment in time, Coop was rocked by the knowledge that it could be the hardest thing he ever had to do when he walked away from her.

IF THE MOMENT OF the kiss had been intense, this moment with Coop holding her close to him was overwhelming. Feelings of being sheltered and protected skimmed past her and didn't have time to settle before she forced herself to push away from him. Awkwardly, she used a large box to her left to steady herself. "I—I'm sorry," she mumbled, not looking directly at Coop. She didn't want to deal with any expression in his dark eyes right then.

Instead, she glanced nervously around at the disarray of the reception foyer. The other times she'd been here, she'd been so focused on her plans, on her vision of what this building could be. But now her focus wasn't extending too far from the man so close to her. Without glancing back at him, she turned and headed for the elevators, picking her way carefully, not about to stumble and take the chance of Coop catching her again.

As she approached the two elevators, with their stark metal doors tarnished and dulled by neglect, she swallowed hard and forced out words: "Winston Lee was considered a minimalist. Clean lines, sweeping spaces. Some people think minimalism means stark or sterile. It can, I suppose, but not with him. He understated everything, so the eye wasn't overwhelmed and could focus on one thing at a time."

She pushed the Up button and was relieved when she heard a whirring. Then, with a groan, the doors on the closest elevator slid open. "I wasn't sure they'd still be working," she said as she stepped into the car. "We'll go all the way up. That's the best part of the whole building—the top floor."

She turned to the front of the car as the doors closed, then moved closer to the sidewall before pushing the button for the fourteenth floor. Normally she hated the canned music they used on elevators, but right now she wished for it. The silence was palpable, and as the car went slowly upward, Dylan stared hard at the control panel beside the door. When Coop finally spoke, she barely kept from jumping.

"No thirteenth floor?" he asked.

She wondered how the man could be asking simple questions, yet his voice seemed almost sensuous. "The top floor's the thirteenth, but superstition lingers on, so it's labeled fourteen. Everyone has their—" Her words broke off abruptly when the elevator lurched to a sudden stop, and the indicator over the door stopped between the tenth and eleventh floor.

No, this couldn't be happening! She reached out and hit the buttons, one after the other, then in frustration when the elevator didn't budge, she hit the top of the panel with the flat of her hand. "Damn it all," she muttered as the air in the car started to thin and become scarce. Coop suddenly grabbed her hand, closed his fingers around hers, and drew her hand back. The action stopped her dead, and she closed her eyes tightly as he murmured, "Don't kill it, or we'll be stuck here forever."

Chapter Six

Forever. Stuck in here with Coop forever. Dylan tried to take deep, even breaths, but couldn't do any better than shaky gasps. "No, it can't do this," she moaned.

His hold on her was tight and sure. "Dylan, it's nothing personal."

Of course, it wasn't. The only personal thing in the elevator was Coop holding her hand, and her inability to break the contact. "I... I meant..." She exhaled unsteadily and opened her eyes as she blurted out, "This has been the worst day of my life."

Coop chuckled softly at that. "I've never been called anyone's worst day before." Then, without any warning, he leaned toward her and brushed a light, teasing kiss across her cool lips.

As his heat fanned her lips, the elevator lurched, gears ground, and the car was moving upward again with a groan. Dylan opened her eyes as Coop drew back. Thankfully he wasn't looking at her, but up, as if he could see through the roof of the elevator car.

"I guess it decided to let us get to the infamous fourteenth floor," he murmured.

He started to look down at her, and she averted her eyes, unable to meet his gaze right then. She grabbed her purse strap with both hands and moved back just enough to get free of his hand. She stared hard at the control panel. "I'm sorry."

"For what?" he asked.

She swallowed hard. "I'm a bit claustrophobic."

"I figured that one out," Coop replied.

She prayed that the elevator would make it to the fourteenth floor smoothly this time with no sudden stops, and she knew if she got the contract, the first thing she would do was put in faster elevators and have a safety system installed. Thankfully, the car stopped at the fourteenth floor, and Dylan barely waited for the doors to open before she stepped out into the reception area.

Taking a deep breath of the musty air, she spoke quickly and nervously as she went forward. "This is the best part of the building." She motioned around in general. "It's unique, all circular, forty feet across. All the wood is solid mahogany." She stopped beside a huge circular desk and knew Coop was right behind her as she gestured overhead to a massive domed skylight. "It's open and has lots of light. When the glass is reglazed, it'll be wonderful, a terrific entry to a series of high level executive offices."

"How about the offices?" Coop asked, his voice echoing strangely in the space and giving the odd impression that it was coming from every direction.

She moved abruptly to one of two corridors that led off the rotunda area and started down the one to the right. The threadbare carpet muffled their footsteps, but she could still hear Coop's pace behind her. Right behind her.

She motioned to the closed side doors as they passed them. "Every office on the west has a fantastic view of the Bay and harbor, every office on the east has a full city and mountain view."

She was sounding more and more like a tour guide all the time, yet with each word, she felt less and less like one. She approached the closed door at the end. "And this office is one of the most terrific of any of them. I think Lee wanted to make a real statement with it, and he did." She touched the tarnished brass handle on the flat wood and pushed it back.

The space behind the doors was so dark there was no suggestion of light at all as Dylan stepped into it. She felt to her left, touched a bank of four light switches and flipped each one until the last one turned on a low light near what had been the reception area for the office behind double doors across the space.

She turned to find Coop silhouetted in the doorway. He was watching her intently, his eyes narrowed, and she knew that the simple act of not being too close to him didn't diminish his effect on her.

He glanced away from her and around the spacious reception area, then back at her. "What's so special in here?"

You, she thought before she could stop the single mental response. She tried to hide from the thought by turning from him and crossing to the inner doors. "Follow me, and I'll show you."

When she opened the doors to a room dappled by moonlight, Coop was right behind her and she knew he saw what was so special when he whistled in appreciation. Across the large shadowy room, stripped bare, was a bank of floor-to-ceiling windows. And beyond the windows was an unobstructed view of the night— the clearing sky, a heavy moon, and the lights of the houses and businesses on the high curve of the bay where ships were anchored on the dark waters.

Coop moved past her, stirring the stale air with the scent that she recognized as unique to him, and she watched him go silently to the windows. The view was secondary to the sight of him as he stopped in front of the glass, his silhouette clearly set against the moonlit night—the definition of the width of his shoulders, the way his hand reached out to touch the glass, his lean hips....

She looked away, feeling embarrassed to be so vulnerable to the sight of a man. Quickly, she moved to the windows, but kept at least three feet of distance from Coop. As she stared out, she made herself talk about things that were growing more and more mundane with each passing moment.

"Winston Lee thought of everything," she said as she reached out to open a section of window in front of her. She was unnerved to realize her hand was slightly unsteady. Then she pushed and the top half of the window swung out a foot to open the room to the night outside. "He...he didn't want to isolate the worker, but to involve the worker," she murmured as the sounds of the city drifted up to them, overlaid with the music from the club nearby.

She heard a click and looked to her left as Coop opened the window in front of him. "A nice touch," he said.

"Especially for a claustrophobic," she added without thinking.

He slanted her a shadowy look and she was thankful for the darkness inside. "You appreciate it, don't you?"

"I really am sorry about that... display in the elevator. Closed spaces bother me a lot, and it was nice to find an architect who opened the inside to the outside world."

"The man liked freedom, didn't he?" Coop asked as he came toward her. She had to fight the urge to back up to keep the buffer between them intact. "No being bound up or shut in or suffocated in any way."

Coop's closeness was doing that very thing, with his presence and his voice, and her breathing was becoming as difficult as it would have been if she'd been put in a four-by-four windowless room.

"You're very perceptive," she said.

"No, I just identify with him a bit. Don't you? Isn't that why you're so enamored of his style?"

She tried not to breathe too deeply, knowing she would only absorb more of the man, only intensify the sensation of drawing his essence into her soul. "I don't know."

He took one last step toward her, and only inches separated them. Ever so slowly, he raised one hand and lightly caressed her cheek with the backs of his fingertips. Dylan couldn't hide a spontaneous shudder, and in the shadows she could see a slight smile play at the corners of his mouth. "Oh, yes, you do," he said softly.

He was so close she felt the heat of his breath brush her face, and she trembled again. "No..." she faltered, but she didn't know what she was objecting to. Whether it was his words, or his touch, or what both were doing to her.

All she knew was that the world seemed to be slowing and everything became breathtakingly clear—his dark eyes on her, the flare of his nostrils with each breath he took, the way his lips were curled with the shadow of a knowing smile; the searing contact of his fingertips on her as they trailed to her jawline, then lightly cupped her chin.

"You want to be able to go whenever you want to go," he whispered unsteadily. "Or as Dylan Briar said, something about staying to enjoy a moment in time when everything lines up, when everything is dead center. Even if it's only for this moment."

Living for the moment. He didn't say the words, but they were there nonetheless. Living for this moment when there was no one else in the world, except Coop and her. This moment when she felt more centered and alive than she ever had. This moment when she was being touched by a man who had come into her life like a blazing comet; a comet that cast startling light, exposing a need in her that she hadn't even known existed until he was there.

"Dance?" he breathed.

She didn't understand the word or the question in it. "Wh-what?"

With a slight inclination of his head, he motioned toward the open windows. "The music," he whispered.

Music was there, the strains of a fifties song "You Send Me," soft and slow on the damp air. She jumped a bit when she felt Coop take her right hand, lacing his fingers lightly with hers. Then his other hand spanned the side of her waist. His eyes held hers and with exquisite slowness, Coop drew her to him.

Her hips met his, and his hand slipped to the small of her back, holding her against him, and without a word, Coop began to move slowly to the music. He drew her hand with his to his chest, and, just the way it had been in the elevator—as if it was the most natural thing in the world—he brushed a kiss across her cheek.

In an old, abandoned office, in a building that time had almost passed by, Dylan realized that a man she had met hours earlier had become the focal point of her life. As she followed his lead, moving to the distant music, the room took on magical proportions.

Live for the moment.

Light and beauty seemed to be everywhere, and she sensed a joining with Coop that had no description. In the darkness they moved together as if they were one, as if they had danced together for a lifetime. And when she let herself rest her cheek in the hollow of his shoulder, she knew a sense of homecoming that defied logic. A stranger, a man who had burst into her life, was starting to feel as if he had been there forever.

She closed her eyes against the sensations, willing them to recede, but all that did was intensify her feelings. She was aware of every place their bodies met, of the way she seemed to fit with him, and she forced her eyes open.

But when she lifted her head from the heat of his shoulder with every intention of stopping what was happening, she met his gaze. The music went on, but they both stopped dancing. Coop uttered a low groan and when the kiss came, it brought with it a wave of white-hot passion that exploded in Dylan.

The passion was born out of a stunning need for this man, and for a heartbeat she couldn't do a thing. She froze, the way she had when he'd kissed her the first time. The feelings were so intense that she could barely absorb them. Then, slowly, she parted her lips and his tongue invaded her, bringing his taste and heat and his own needs.

She lifted her arms, circling his neck, straining to be closer, almost wishing she had the ability to dissolve into him, to feel him all around her, to experience him in a way she had never experienced another man. When his hands slipped down to her hips and drew her tightly against him, the intimacy felt searing. She knew that his feelings echoed her own. She could feel his hard strength against her, and his low moan vibrated deep in her soul.

Live for the moment.

She was doing just that, and it frightened her more than just a bit. Despite the feelings that swamped her, she couldn't get past the knowledge that this shouldn't be happening—not here, not now, not with a stranger. A stranger who could touch her and find her soul. A stranger who had the ability to bring a life to her that she had never suspected was hidden in her. A stranger who could make her do things she had never done before—throw caution to the wind, want more, need more. A stranger.

That echoed in her, and with it came a certain chill that began to douse the fire that was building in her. A stranger.

With a gasp, she drew back, awkwardly disengaging her hold on Coop, and he didn't fight her. He let her go and suddenly she was isolated. She felt alone in the dark, even though he was mere inches from her; even though she could hear his ragged breathing and all but inhale the heat that had built between them. Yet she was cut off, with no contact, and the sense of loss was startling.

It was all she could do not to reach out in the darkness for him again. She clenched her hands so tightly that her nails bit into her palms and she tried to take steadying breaths. Fortunately the music changed right then, going from slow and romantic, to a rock-and-roll hit.

Without a word he reached out, and it was all she could do not to flinch when he touched her chin with one finger. "Time to go?" he asked, his voice rough and unsteady and thankfully not saying anything about "lesson three." She didn't need him to point that out to her, or to remind how miserably she failed the test.

She was shaking when she whispered, "Yes," and broke the contact as she turned and headed for the open door. There was nothing to do but leave, and not even try to make sense of a day that bordered on insanity.

BY THE TIME COOP DROVE back to Dylan's house, the tension in him had made his shoulders ache and his neck tight. He'd never felt a need for a woman like he did for Dylan. He could admit that now. As soon as he'd held her in his arms, he'd known the naked truth of that.

But what he would never have guessed was the fact that what he needed from her went beyond the basic physical desires that were so obvious. He didn't understand that at all. She was beautiful, intelligent, fascinating, and desirable. He understood that much, but what else was it he needed from her? As he pulled into her driveway he flexed his fingers, trying to ease their deathlike grip on the steering wheel.

When the car came to a stop, Dylan opened the door without a word and got out. Coop hurried after her through the courtyard and up to the entry to her home, intending to say goodbye and leave. She'd stopped everything at the office, and he wasn't going to press her. He'd never done that before and he certainly wouldn't start it with a woman like Dylan. But when she opened the door to her darkened house and turned to him, he knew he couldn't just let it go. He couldn't walk away and lose whatever it was that was happening between them.

"What now?" he asked, desperately wanting an answer that made sense.

She shrugged with a fluttery, uncertain motion of her slender shoulders. "I...I don't know. We've hardly met, but..." Even in the night, he could see her tongue touch her lips, an endearing and disturbing habit that he'd recognized in her. A habit that touched him on a raw, basic level. "It's just...I've never had anything like this happen before," she whispered.

"I'm not sure I have, either," he admitted softly. "But does that mean it can't happen?"

She retreated half a step and he could tell her back must be against the doorjamb. She exhaled softly, then said, "That's just it. I don't know what 'it' is."

"Do we have to understand it, or can we just enjoy whatever's happening?"

He knew that sounded shallow as soon as the words were said, but he didn't mean it that way. His feelings for Dylan were anything but shallow, and maybe that was why he couldn't turn and leave. He'd never been one to sidestep a risk, and a part of him knew that staying was a risk. But it was a risk he wanted to take.

"Then you go your way, and I go mine?" she suggested.

That sounded cold and clinical. "Maybe it's more like a moment out of time, a pause in our lives. I'm probably going to Europe tomorrow and you'll be off making Winston Lee's buildings come alive again. I just know that what's happening here and now doesn't happen every day—at least it doesn't for me."

She was the one to laugh now, with a soft, gentle sound that drew him to her like a moth to a flame. He moved closer, aching to feel her under his hands again, to taste her and hold her. But he made himself not reach out—not yet. He took a shaky breath and forced out words that he knew he had to say, but that didn't stop him from wishing he didn't. "If you want me to go, I'll go. Just say so."

She stood in the shadows for what seemed an eternity before he heard her exhale on a sigh. Finally, she reached out and took his hand, lacing her fingers with his and holding on so tightly he could feel her trembling. Then she drew him into the house with her. Only when the door shut behind them did she let go of his hand and turn to him in the shadows.

"Are you sure?" he asked.

"I don't want you to leave." She didn't want him to walk away and out of her life—not yet. And as he framed her face with the heat of his hands, she knew she was just starting "lesson number four" in living for the moment.

His thumbs slowly stroked her cheeks as he whispered roughly, "I don't want to leave."

Dylan covered Coop's hands with hers and knew she was in way over her head with this man. For a moment she thought she understood what he'd told her about looking at danger and getting a rush. She knew she was looking at danger right now, and excitement, anticipation and fear mingled in her.

"Then, stay," she breathed.

He was motionless, his thumbs stilling on her skin. Without looking away, he brushed his hands over her hair, then slowly took the pins out. As her hair fell free around her shoulders, Coop came even closer, leaning down, but not kissing her. "Are you sure?"

She touched her trembling lips with her tongue and managed to whisper, "Yes, yes."

With a low moan, he captured her lips with his. Passion and need ignited in her, searing through her, and she lost herself in the circle of his arms, in the taste of his mouth ravishing hers, in the sensations of him surrounding her. Time might not be able to stop, but for now, for this night, it had no meaning. Whatever came tomorrow, she would deal with it. She would go on, but for tonight, this was her moment.

Dylan circled his neck with her arms, holding Coop, arching against him. The kiss was more than a simple caress. It was a possession, a branding, and she welcomed it. Reason was gone, sanity a thing of the past, and she lived in that moment, letting it consume her.

There was no gentle building of passion. It was already there, white-hot and all-consuming, rocking Dylan and filling her with a need to touch and explore Coop that was like a physical hunger. She drew her hands around to his chest and awkwardly tried to undo the buttons on his shirt, needing that skin-to-skin contact.

His fingers tangled in her hair and when his mouth released hers, his lips burned a path to the side of her throat, tasting the sensitive area by her ear.

A button popped as she tugged to get it free of the hole, then the last button was gone and she worked her hands under the cotton. His skin was sleek and warm, and as she pressed her palms to his chest, she felt his heart hammering against his ribs.

She ran her hands over him, feeling his nipples harden, then his hands found her. He lowered a hand to her hips, then up to her waist and under her sweater. His touch inflamed her skin, making her gasp, then his hands were on her breasts, and even through the thin lace of her bra, her response was immediate and intense.

She arched back when warm waves of pleasure washed over her as his thumb and forefinger teased her nipple, causing sensations to coil deep in her being. With a low whimper, she leaned toward him, pressing a kiss to the hollow of his throat. She felt his voice rumble against her lips as he whispered hoarsely, "The bedroom?"

"Back... All the way back," she said, her voice muffling against his skin.

The next thing she knew, he swept her off the floor, cradling her easily in his arms, and as she circled his neck with her arms, she looked up into his shadowy face. She had known him hours, just hours, yet she felt more connected to him than she ever had to any man who had been in her life before.

She pressed her cheek to his chest. *More connected and more alive and more needy.* She closed her eyes tightly as he carried her through the darkness of the hallway. Then she heard a thump and opened her eyes as the door to her bedroom swung back.

Moonlight bathed the room in rippling light and shadow, showing the outline of the four-poster bed opposite the French doors. Coop carried her to the bed, then she was on the comforter, getting to her knees and facing him, almost at eye level with him on the high mattress. Without a word he slipped off his shirt, then his jeans were gone and he was in front of her in just his undershorts.

She couldn't move. She couldn't do anything but simply look at him. Moonlight bathed him, etching stark shadows against the light planes of his body—a hard, lean body. And the moonlight exposed his need of her that was obviously as great as her need of him.

His eyes were shadowed, but she knew he was studying her, skimming his gaze over her. Then he reached out to her. His hands found the hem of her sweater and gently tugged it up and over her head. He tossed it back over his shoulder, his gaze never leaving her, and without even a touch from him, her breasts tingled and she could feel her nipples responding as if he'd kissed them.

There was no embarrassment, no urge to cover herself, as Dylan reached behind her, unsnapped the clasp of her bra and pulled the fine lace aside.

"God, you're beautiful," he said with a low groan, then reached out to her, his hands skimming over her sensitive nipples. "Beautiful."

Pleasure didn't begin to define what Dylan experienced from his touch. It went beyond simple pleasure into a totally new realm—the sensations surrounded her, ran through her, possessed her. Then she reached out to him and he came to her.

Together they fell back onto the bed, then he was there with her, lying by her, and control had vanished. The rest of their clothes were gone before she even realized it, and they lay face-to-face in the tangled comforter, in the moonlight and shadows. Their hands explored and their mouths tasted, over and over again, urgent and demanding, as if they could never get enough of the sensations, the startling newness of everything.

The moment exploded with ecstasy as Coop slid his hand over her stomach and down to the center of her being. His hand covered her, pressing against her, then with slow circles, he brought a response from her that was both wanton and frightening. She moved against his touch, arching, exposing herself in a way that seemed so intimate and yet so natural.

Sensations started to build into an almost-painful knot that begged for release, and just when she was certain she would explode, his touch was gone. But before she could cry out, he was over her, bracing himself with his hands by her shoulders, his dark eyes burning into hers. She felt his velvet strength touch her—testing, tentative, until she arched her hips against him and circled his neck with her arms, pulling him toward her.

Then, with exquisite slowness, he filled her until they were joined completely. Neither of them moved. The feelings were too intense, too close to the surface, and Dylan was sure if there was one movement, she would shatter from it. But when Coop eased partly out, then thrust back in again, she met his stroke and knew how wrong she had been.

The pleasure just grew and grew, building beyond anything she had ever dreamed a person could feel. And as the rhythm sped up, as the need grew more urgent, she felt herself going into a place where there was just herself and Coop. Just the two of them, their touching, their joining. Then the explosion came. Shards of beauty and completeness were everywhere, and at the peak, Dylan cried out, her voice mingling with Coop's, and the two were one for that moment in time.

Chapter Seven

Dylan held on to Coop as they drifted back to reality together, and she never let go, even when he left her and pulled her to his side. She laid her head against the hot dampness of his chest and as her breathing settled, she spread her hand over his abdomen. Cradled in the safety of his arms, she let herself drift. There was nothing shocking to her now, nothing touched with regret. And in that moment when she was falling into the soft cocoon of sleep, she felt Coop brush a kiss across her forehead.

The contact was so slight, so undemanding, and yet in that moment, she saw everything with clarity. She'd made love with this man, and as sleep surrounded her, she realized that the word *love* was so close to the truth that she couldn't even look at it right then.

She snuggled against him, exhaled on a sigh, and let sleep claim her. She could stay here in the grayness, hold on to him, and be in his arms without having to think about anything right now.

She woke slowly, finding her way out of a place of perfect contentment. But the closer she got to consciousness, the more her middle tightened. She began to feel heat at her back, a hand around her, touching her with incredible intimacy just under her breasts, and a thigh resting heavily across her own. It was then she knew just how much out of control she'd allowed her once sane life to become; just how far she'd let herself get lost in living for the moment.

When a deep, male sigh near her ear fanned her skin with shimmering heat, she scrunched her eyes so tightly that colors exploded behind her lids. She stayed very still, while every uncertainty that she'd forced away the night before come back with the force of a fist in her stomach.

Coop. A stranger, yet a man who had drawn things out of her that she hadn't even realized she'd been capable of doing. A man who had touched her in a way that had exploded reason and sanity, who had brought exquisite pleasure and something else. She sought for the word, then it came with blinding clarity and it made her tremble. He was a man who could love a woman with a beauty that was breathtaking.

Love. The word was there again, but had barely formed when she felt Coop stir, then whisper, "Are you awake?"

She almost pretended to be sleeping, knowing that once she moved, the barriers would be gone again. Then she would be lost again. But when his hand gently cupped her breast, there was no pretense left in her. The low moan as his fingers found her nipple was real enough, and when his lips pressed to her shoulder, she gave up completely. She covered his hand with hers and took a shuddering breath.

"I thought so," he murmured against her skin. "Shh, listen."

She had been listening to her own heart starting to pound, and the sound of his breathing in her ears. But now she became aware of the rain outside, the soft whisper of the drops against the windows. "Raining again," she murmured. "I can't remember the last time it rained for Halloween."

As his hand teased her nipple into a hard bud and sensations shot through her, he whispered close to her ear, "I've never really liked rain...until now."

His hand shifted to her shoulder and gently eased her back toward him, and as she turned, she saw him over her. Shadows softened everything except her feelings for the man, and the ache of need deep inside. "I don't know how this all happened," she said, admitting a stark truth. "I still don't understand it."

He brushed the hair back from her face, the tips of his fingers trailing down along her cheek to her jaw, then coming to rest on the rapid pulse in the hollow of her throat. "One thing I've learned in this life is to go with the flow. Don't look for answers when they aren't there." He kissed her—a hard, fierce contact—then drew back and exhaled in a rush. "Now is all there is. Now...here."

"And what about tomorrow?"

His fingers moved to her lips, in a caress as light as a feather, but as unsteady as her own heartbeat. "There's just now," he whispered roughly. "Tomorrow never comes. Lesson number five. Okay?"

For the first time in her life Dylan let tomorrow go and knew that this was really all she had—all she would ever have with Coop—and she wanted it. She wanted it with a passion that knew no bounds, and silently she circled his neck and drew him back down to her. "Okay."

Their coming together earlier had been intense and painfully filled with hunger. But this time when he came to her, it was slow and leisurely, as if they were trying to make it last as long as they possibly could. Dylan touched and felt Coop, almost memorizing the sensations of his skin, the muscles and heat, trying to burn the images into her mind. As something to keep, something to have in her heart when the man was long gone.

When he turned onto his back, lifting her easily to sit astride him, he lowered her onto his strength, and the pleasure was so intense it was almost painful. But she hesitated, not moving, so she could absorb the sensations that rocked her. Then Coop spanned her waist and raised his hips.

All the sense of having endless time was gone. Urgent passion cut through Dylan and burned into her soul. She felt consumed, as if Coop could absorb her and she could fit into his being. She called out, her voice mingling with his, then the world shattered into nothing but pleasure and the man who was with her.

There was no one else, nothing else in the universe but that moment, that heartbeat when the joining was complete. All she had was the moment. And right then, it was enough.

COOP WOKE TO BRIGHT SUN across his closed eyes, and he knew instantly where he was and who was snuggled into his side. God, he'd never experienced anything like this before, and for the first time he considered what it would be like to wake with Dylan every morning; what it would be like to go to sleep with her every night.

But as soon as the thought formed, he pushed it aside. It didn't make sense. Just because Dylan was special and the night had been more than unique, that didn't change the basic premise of his life.

He opened his eyes, shifting slightly to avoid the glare of sunlight streaming in through the French doors across the room from the four-poster bed. He saw the blur of her hair on his shoulder, and absorbed the feeling of her hand resting just over his heart. He knew this was it, but he wasn't about to cut it short. He lay very still, letting her sleep, just letting the moment stretch for as long as it could. Maybe today there would be more time for them. Maybe he wouldn't hear from Brokaw until tomorrow.

But then maybe he would, he thought with pointed logic. But he could stay until then, and if he stayed, he would have to leave a number where Brokaw could reach him. He braced himself, then eased his arm out from under Dylan. She sighed, then rolled onto her side and settled back into sleep.

Carefully he slipped out of bed, looked around, then saw a phone in a sitting area to the right of the French doors. Quietly he crossed the cool wooden floor and reached for the cordless phone on a glass-topped table by a side window. He called the hotel, and in a low voice identified himself. A man with a disgustingly bright voice said he was glad he was calling in; they had an urgent message for him.

While the man put him on hold to go and get the message, Coop turned to look back into the bedroom, at Dylan in the bed. The sight of her almost hurt. Her hair was dark against the ivory pillow cases, and the sheets clung to the curve of her hips. He could feel his body responding to the sight of her, and it was jarring when the man came back on the line.

"Here it is, sir. 'Everything is ready. Time to get to work. Call me as soon as you get this. We need you at the test site in twenty-four hours. Brokaw.'"

Coop swallowed hard before hanging up. The phone had barely been put back in the cradle when it rang, with a sharp disturbing sound. Coop glanced at Dylan and saw her shift, turning onto her back as her eyelids fluttered. Then her sleep filled eyes met his across the space.

How was he going to tell her that the call had come, that he had to leave in just a few hours? The impact of her gaze meeting his was startling, and he knew he wasn't going to simply leave. They could talk, spend more time together, and maybe figure out where to go from here. He watched her brush at her hair, then a small smile flitted across her lips.

God, she was the most beautiful thing he'd ever seen. And the most desirable. Even as the phone rang beside him, he realized that he didn't have to walk away, that he didn't have to lose whatever was happening here. He knew how much she wanted that contract, and he knew it was selfish. But if she didn't get the contract, he could ask her to come to Europe with him for a while.

"The phone," she murmured.

He never looked away from her, his decision settling in him. Yes, she could come with him. He touched the phone, lifted it and said, "Yes?"

"Is Ms. Bradford there, please? It's Colin Dytmyer calling."

"Just a minute." He looked at Dylan. "A Colin Dytmyer."

She stared at him for a long moment, her expression unreadable, then she said a soft, "Oh, yes," and scrambled to sit up. The sheets fell back and Coop tightened his hold on the receiver to the breaking point when he was faced with the sight of her half naked. Her breasts tempted him, and it was all he could do to calmly walk over to the bed and stand over her, holding the receiver out to her.

"Thanks," she murmured and reached for the phone.

Her hand brushed his as she took the receiver, and he killed the impulse to hold on to her. Then the contact was gone, and she was talking on the phone.

"Dylan Bradford, here."

He watched her—the nervous way she smoothed her tangled hair, the lack of embarrassment at her partial nakedness, and the way she closed her eyes as the person on the other end of the line spoke to her. He could imagine what they could do in Europe. He loved it there—the beaches, the small, secluded spots where he'd gone many times for R and R. But now, images of making love to Dylan in each and every one of those places superseded anything else.

Her tongue touched her lips, and he dropped down on the bed beside her, his need for contact too long unsatisfied. He touched her bare shoulder, and he could feel her jump. Then her eyes opened and he looked into their navy depths.

"Yes, sir, that's wonderful," she said, her gaze never leaving his. "Yes. Of course."

He leaned toward her and laid a kiss by his hand on her shoulder, loving the way she trembled slightly in response. She tasted wonderful. Moving closer, he slid his hand to the nape of her neck, letting his fingers tangle in the dark mane, and he found a spot behind her ear with his lips.

He was far from letting go. He knew that and was startled by a following thought that he didn't want to let go. That was new for him. The letting go had been a part of his makeup all of his life—until now. He knew it would come, but not for a while, a long while.

"Yes, I guess that's okay," she whispered into the phone, angling her head to one side to expose more of her throat to him. "Yes, I will."

Coop tasted her, skimming over the silky heat, and when they both fell back into the bed together, he pulled her to him. Her leg wrapped around his, tangling with the sheets, and her free hand touched his chest.

"Yes, sir. I will. And thank you."

Coop drew back, raising himself on one elbow to look down at her. She turned off the phone, then tossed it, without looking, into the pillows behind her head. Then her arms came up and circled his neck. "Good morning," she whispered.

He took a quick, fierce kiss, then drew back and smiled down at her. "Good morning. No rain, and it's a wonderful day."

"Fabulous," she breathed with a slow, stunning smile.

He laid his free hand on her middle, spanning her diaphragm with his fingers, relishing the feel of her trembling under his touch. "I think there's something that could make it even better."

She moved closer still, her hips against his, and there were no secrets about what his body wanted. "I know. Me, too, but there's something I need to tell you."

He moved his hand higher, cupping her breast, and the nipple was already aroused. "What's that?"

"The call ... Mr. Dytmyer?"

"The old boyfriend?" he asked as he teased her nipple between his thumb and forefinger.

She gasped and covered his hand with hers to still his action. "No, he's not an old boyfriend."

He lowered his head to touch her nipple with his lips, and was startled when she drew back from him. He looked down at her and she framed his face with both hands. "Coop, listen to me."

"Sure. Just don't take too long."

"Mr. Dytmyer, he's with the city and he's the one who got the final bids on the contract." She exhaled, then smiled brilliantly. "I've got it. I've got it!"

He stared down at her and felt a cutting chill invade the bed. "You got it?"

"The contract," she breathed, then she was hugging him, her hold trembling, and he knew that the best-laid plans of anyone crumbled sooner or later. He pressed a kiss to her silky hair and whispered, "Congratulations. I knew you could do it." He held her tightly to him and closed his eyes. "That's wonderful. It's your dream come true."

Dylan buried her face in the heat of Coop's naked chest. Her dream come true. She'd done it. Really done it.

Slowly she moved back so she could face Coop, and she knew that her dreams *had* come true. Dreams she hadn't even known she had until she met Coop. She had the contract and Coop was in her life. "Yes, everything's working out."

"Congratulations," he whispered again.

Then she realized that the word was right, but the tone wasn't. It sounded flat, as if it was difficult for him to say, and her impulse to hold on to him and share this moment with him was killed by the look in his eyes.

She touched his face, feeling the bristling of a new beard starting. "Is . . . is something wrong?"

He shook his head. "No, nothing. Everything's just the way it should be," he said, then kissed her again. But that was wrong too. His lips lingered on hers, yet the passion was held at bay. It was all wrong.

Then he drew back, still touching her face, and she could feel a slight unsteadiness in his touch. "Coop, what's going on?"

"You've got your contract, and my clearance came through today. I called in to the hotel and Brokaw had left a message for me. I've got a five-year contract. And I have to meet him right after lunch."

She'd been living for this phone call from Dytmyer. But now that it had come, the incredible happiness she'd talked to Tori about was held at bay. There had been real happiness for her, but she had the flashing thought that it had come last night, in the darkness with Coop. She touched her tongue to her lips. "What now?"

He rolled away from her onto his back and stared up at the ceiling. "What do we have, a few hours before I need to leave?"

"I have to meet Dytmyer at eleven."

"What now?"

She wanted to say she wanted him to make love to her one more time, to just hold her and stay there forever, but that didn't make sense. She moved closer, lying on her stomach and resting her hand on his shoulder, then her chin on her hand. "Live for the moment?" she whispered.

He glanced at her, his eyes smoldering, yet edged with something that could have been pain. "That's all it can be right now," he breathed.

"I know."

With a low moan, he came to her. His touch on her was so familiar and so painfully needed that Dylan met him with a hunger that defied description.

The contact was devastating, his body over hers, her responses so intimate and basic that tears were there before she even knew they were forming. She clung to Coop, tasting him, touching him, pulling him to her and into her, and lifting her hips higher as if she could will him deeper into her. Then the movement began, hard and driven, and it filled her with ecstasy that exploded almost before it had begun.

Dylan clutched the moment, and the tears increased when she felt it start to fade. But the luxury of slowly falling back to reality wasn't meant to be right then. Coop kissed her lightly, then he was gone.

She swiped at her eyes and grabbed the sheets for cover. As she saw Coop walk naked to where his clothes lay in a heap on the floor, she bit her lip so hard she could almost taste the blood on her tongue.

"We can do something this afternoon, after you see Brokaw—something wonderful and special," she said in a devastatingly unsteady voice.

"I'm leaving as soon as I see Brokaw," he returned abruptly as he grabbed his jeans. "Brokaw's in a hurry to get going on the project. I have to fly out right away."

She watched him step into his pants and tried to think of something else. "There has to be some way to do this."

He turned as he zipped up his fly, and his expression seemed tight. "I don't see how."

She scrambled off the bed, grabbed her robe and slipped on the navy terry-cloth cover-up, then watched while Coop put on his shirt. As he tugged it down and tucked it into his waistband with quick, sharp strokes, she spoke without thinking: "I never thought this would happen."

He glanced across the mussed bed at her, then raked his fingers through his hair, spiking it slightly. "That makes two of us."

"Don't you get any time off?"

He leaned against the far post at the foot of the bed and put on his socks and shoes. "It'll be at least a year to get the project off the ground before I can take a break." He slowly straightened and studied her where she stood by the side of the bed. "How about you? Will you start work right away?"

"I think so. They seem to be in a rush now that they've made the decision." She grasped at straws. "Maybe I could put Dytmyer off for a few hours, and we could—"

As she spoke, he came around the bed to her, but didn't touch her. Instead, he smiled, an expression touched with a shadow of regret. "No, don't. We can't," he said softly. "You need to make that meeting, and I need to make mine. I'm sorry."

So was she, deep in her soul. Very sorry. "Then we... I..."

"Exactly," he whispered. Then he bent to her and touched his lips to hers.

The kiss was short and far from sweet, when what she really wanted was to hold on to him and pull him back into the bed with her and never let him go. But when she moved closer, he stepped back and caught both of her hands in his. "No, if we start anything else, neither one of us will make our appointments." He shook his head. "That can't happen."

She laced her fingers in his. "You...you have a safe flight to Europe."

He hesitated, then let her go long enough to frame her face with both of his hands. "You know, you're going to be just fine, Dylan Bradford." He brushed his thumbs lightly over her cheeks. "You'll make those damn buildings beautiful again, and you'll go on to bigger and better things. I can promise you that."

All she could do was stare at him, storing up the image for a future when he wouldn't be around. "We can't lose contact. I mean, we could call and—" She touched her tongue to her lips. "A phone number?"

"No, I won't have one. It's all top security, but I can call you. I will." He closed his eyes for a brief moment, then said, "Listen, I think I might be able to take a break in January, just after New Year's. I can try to get back here for a few days then. Can I take a rain check on the tour-guide thing until then?"

She nodded, and he pulled her to him. She rubbed her forehead against his chest, against the beating of his heart, then slowly he held her back. For a long, hard moment his eyes burned into hers; then he kissed her one last time—a quick, fierce contact that rocked her.

As he let her go, he whispered, "Until January." Then he turned toward the door to leave.

She closed her eyes tightly and heard his footsteps on the hardwood floors, going down the corridor, getting fainter and fainter. Then the front door opened and closed.

When Dylan heard his car start, she sank down on the bed and when she opened her eyes, she averted her gaze from the rumpled sheets as memories bombarded her.

"Until January," she whispered to the empty room.

Chapter Eight

Christmas Eve
San Diego

"I'm sorry I'm late," Dylan gasped as she hurried into Tori's home, a bungalow in the hills just east of the city. "I had to make sure the match for the molding in the rotunda was right." She quickly took off her coat, tossed it on the bench in the small entryway, then went into the living room.

"I meant to get back earlier to help with the tree...." Her voice trailed off when she saw the Christmas tree by the windows, fully decorated with white angels, red apples and red and white lights that hadn't been turned on yet. Tori was on her knees adjusting presents under the tree, and she turned to Dylan where she stood in the doorway.

Tori stood and brushed at her jeans and top. She was slender again after having had the baby, and without any makeup on, she looked like a teenager. "So, do the moldings match?"

Dylan grimaced. "Sorry, but I just couldn't leave until it was settled. I guess I'm late."

"Very," Allan said as he came into the room carrying the baby. Dylan looked at A.J., tiny and pink, with a mop of dark hair, suffering the indignity of wearing oversize Santa sleepers and a stocking cap. He fit in Allan's arms as if he had been made just for that spot. "A.J. took a powder about an hour ago waiting for you to show up," he said, motioning to the sleeping baby.

Dylan studied the tiny face barely visible around a huge pacifier that she could see, moving rhythmically, from where she stood. She'd missed the baby being born by an hour because she couldn't get away from a meeting with Dytmyer. And she'd kept her distance ever since, admiring him from afar and saying the right things about how cute he was, even though he had the decided look of a gnome.

"I'm sorry," she said as she sank down in an easy chair near the tree. She'd been so tired all day, barely keeping herself going, and she'd felt squeamish off and on. Too much work. Too little sleep. Too much stress.

So when Allan approached and acted as if he was going to put A.J. in her arms, she recoiled. "I'm...I'm sick, I think," she said quickly.

"You look fine, maybe a bit thin, but fine," Allan said as he stooped to ease the baby into her awkward hold.

She sat ramrod straight holding her nephew as she looked imploringly at Tori. "Tori, I don't think—"

Tori cut her off with a sweep of her hand. "You need to get to know him, Dylan. He's not an ornament. Do some bonding. He won't break, and besides, you need the practice for when you have your own."

"Tori, I—"

"I know, I know," she muttered as she straightened out the extension cord for the lights. "You're too busy for that. *And* you aren't interested. *And* there isn't anyone in your life right now. I know all your excuses."

Dylan sat very still, swallowing hard when her stomach lurched. She couldn't decide if she felt sick from the lack of food today, or from the way the image of Coop could come to her with a clarity that made her slightly light-headed. He'd been gone two months, and during that time there had only been three phone calls—awkward yet very welcome times of talking about inconsequential things.

He would be back in January. And of course there were her memories—the way she could almost see him when she woke in the morning; or that flashing moment when she thought she saw him when she would walk into the offices on the top floor of the Santa Clare building.

"Not excuses," she muttered.

"So, how's it going at the buildings?" Allan asked, and she knew he was asking to distract Tori, not because he was really interested.

"It's moving along quickly," she said. "They want it ready by next September." A.J. moved suddenly, stretching one hand hidden by the sleeve of the Santa suit over his head, and he yawned. Just when Dylan thought he was settling back down, she saw his eyelids flutter, then she was being regarded by squinting eyes of an indeterminate color.

She wished she had the knack of talking to babies, but all she could do was look back at him, praying he would go back to sleep. Instead, he started to fidget, and before she could tell Tori to take him, he scrunched his eyes shut and let out a cry that could have stirred the dead. His face went bright red, his hand shook and his tiny chin trembled.

"Tori?" she called over the noise as she noticed that Allan was nowhere to be seen.

"He's got gas. Allan let him go to sleep right after I nursed him," she said as she got on her hands and knees to reach under the tree to plug in the lights. "Put him on your shoulder and burp him."

Awkwardly Dylan maneuvered A.J. onto her shoulder, then tapped his back once. There was a burp, but that wasn't all. It was followed by a choking sound, then Dylan felt wet warmth spread over her shoulder. At the same time she saw and smelled curdled milk all over her sweater, Tori was there to grab the baby. Dylan felt her own stomach clench horribly.

She scrambled to her feet, grabbing a receiving blanket Allan held out to her as he came back into the room, and ran for the bathroom just off the entry-way. She barely made it inside when waves of nausea hit her with a vengeance. She grabbed the porcelain sides of the toilet, dropped to her knees, and was sicker than she'd ever been in her entire life.

When the spasms finally subsided, she sank back on her knees and reached for a towel from the vanity. Pressing the terry cloth to her face, she closed her eyes and waited out another wave of nausea. Her stomach was empty, and her sides hurt. But for that moment the sickness was gone.

"What's going on?" Tori asked from somewhere behind her.

Dylan wiped her face with the towel, then exhaled. "I told you I was sick. I feel horrible."

"I thought you were just run-down because of all the work you've been doing."

"It's the flu."

Tori was right there and pressed her warm hand to Dylan's forehead. "Nope, no fever."

"It is so. Everyone's getting it, but I can't afford to get sick. I've got a million things to do, and they've put such a rush on this project I'm always five steps behind, as it is. And I'm exhausted all the time."

Dylan slowly got to her feet, then looked at Tori by the sink. Her sister was staring at her with a look that Dylan knew well. It was that smug expression of infi-nite understanding, as if she knew the secrets of the ages and was just waiting for someone to ask her about them.

"What?" she muttered as she tossed the towel into the sink. "Just say what you're thinking."

"I was just trying to figure out how long ago we had the accident?"

The statement came out of nowhere and made Dylan catch her breath sharply. There wasn't a time when Coop couldn't slip into her mind like that, with an ease that defied explanation. She reached for the faucet and turned on cold water, letting it run over her hands. "It was the day before Halloween. Why?" she asked, looking at her sister's reflection in the mirror.

Their eyes met. "I was just wondering."

Dylan could feel her stomach starting to churn again. "Why?"

"Allan said he saw you and Mr. Reeves together in the waiting room, that he was holding you by the arm and that you left the hospital with him."

Dylan closed her eyes tightly and took a shaky breath. *Live for the moment. Tomorrow never comes.* "He was very nice about everything," she whispered.

"You never said much about him, except you expect him to be back in San Diego sometime after the New Year."

"That's what he said."

"You did more than just show him around the city, didn't you?"

Despite her sickness, Dylan felt her face grow hot. "He . . . he was really understanding."

"And?"

"Okay, he and I . . . We hit it off."

"Is that what they call it now?"

"Oh, Tori, for—"

"Dylan , the last time I felt the way you're feeling, I was pregnant."

Dylan's eyes flew open to her image in the mirror. She looked pale and tired, and shock made her mouth look tight. She'd been sick. She had the flu. She was overworked and tired. That was all there was to it. Besides, they'd used protection.

"No," she breathed.

"You didn't sleep with him?"

There was Coop's image in her mind, so vivid she felt as if she could reach out and touch him. And she wanted to feel his reality right then, so they—the two people on earth who didn't even relate to kids and possibly hated them—could both laugh at what Tori was suggesting.

Pregnant?

There was no laughter in her as she slowly let go of the sink and pressed her palms to her stomach. "I...I can't be pregnant." She stared at her hands. "We were careful."

"You know there's an error rate with anything like that, don't you? Nothing's absolutely sure, except abstinence."

"Tori, I don't need a lecture on the fallibility of birth-control methods," she muttered.

Tori reached around her and fumbled in the medicine cabinet, then turned with a box in her hand. "I was using these all the time when I was trying to get pregnant with A.J." She held it out to Dylan. "If I were you, I'd want to know for sure."

She stared at the box that held a pregnancy-test kit, and all she wanted was to feel all right and for January to come. But that wasn't going to happen today. She took the box from her sister. "If it's positive, then what?" she whispered.

"Tell the father when he comes back in January."

Coop had told her about his life; what he wanted and what he didn't want. And he didn't want children. "He doesn't like kids at all," Dylan said softly. Just the idea of a child had broken up his marriage, and what she and Coop had had was far more tenuous than any marriage. "He said he's even worse with kids than I would be."

Tori touched her cold cheek. "You'd be terrific. You just don't know it yet. And maybe you're underestimating him."

She looked up at Tori and said flatly, "You're overestimating me. I'm not mother material. I never have been."

"Dylan—"

"I don't *want* to be."

"People change."

"Tori, I won't change. I don't want to be pregnant, and I don't want to have a child, and I don't want to be a mother. And when Coop gets here in January, I don't want to hit him with any news about me being pregnant."

Her voice was rising with each word, and Tori hushed her. "Now, now, now. Don't get so upset. Just take the test, and maybe you won't have to say anything to him when he gets here."

"Okay," she replied. "Just let me get this over with." She opened the box with annoyingly unsteady fingers, trying to push any thoughts of Coop out of her mind as she dumped the contents of the box onto the side of the sink.

Right then she heard A.J. crying loudly somewhere down the hall, and Tori studied her intently as the crying got louder. "What *are* you going do if this comes out positive?"

Dylan swallowed a surge of nausea and muttered, "I don't know," and reached for the tiny plastic cup. "Just tell me what to do."

New Year's Eve
Southern Spain

"YOU PUSHED IT TOO HARD!" Brokaw called over the roar of the motor as Coop took off his safety helmet. Then he made a motion for Coop to cut the engine of the sleek, gray metal prototype car.

The dark-haired man given to wearing his long hair in a ponytail was dressed in jeans and a black polo shirt. His angular face with its shaggy mustache was tugged into a frown. When the motor died, he leaned forward and gripped the frame of the empty driver's window. "Did you hear what I said?" he asked intently.

"Of course I did, and I was doing my job, Brokaw," Coop muttered as he raked his fingers through his hair. "The job that you and the big boys are paying me a lot of money to do, I might point out."

"You're crazy. Pure and simple. You aren't doing this for the money. You never have. You do it for the rush. I know that. But lately you've seemed reckless—and that's a real problem."

Coop glanced at the man with the dust of the test track streaking the reds and oranges of the setting sun at his back. Brokaw was annoying him, getting on nerves that were already wound tight. "I'm supposed to push these damn machines. And I am. That's why we call it testing. If you want someone else, go for it, and I'm out of here."

Brokaw shook his head. "That's not what I'm saying, Coop." He tried to make a joke to break the growing tension. "Of course, when it comes to driving a Mercedes on the city streets, you stink."

Coop found a smile at that when the words conjured up images of Dylan. Dylan in the rain. Dylan in the shadows. Dancing. Touching. Dylan in his arms. Dylan that last morning. He shook his head sharply. "Yeah, I stink at mundane things. I always have. That's why I avoid them like the plague."

"*And* you've got nothing to lose."

Coop felt an odd tightness in his chest at Brokaw's words. Since he'd left San Diego, he'd wondered how true that was. He never stopped thinking about Dylan, and when they talked, just her voice made him feel an odd connection that he'd never experienced before. Just hearing her voice distracted him, and he hadn't called her for over two weeks because he hadn't been sure he could have stayed in Spain until this phase was done. Thoughts of her possessed him and drew him, and a phone call was no substitute for actually seeing her.

He would do that in January. He would go back and see if it was all memory and imagination, or if what he remembered was real. They had a date, and he was going to keep it.

"What I'm losing is the light. Let's do one more run, then you can go and party in the New Year," Coop said. He reached for his helmet, tugged it back on and clicked in the mouthpiece that recorded his observations during the test.

He wasn't doing this for one last thrill. He owed it to Brokaw. If he'd been concentrating on the last run, he probably could have pinpointed the reason for the shimmy.

But he'd been thinking about other things, about rain and night and making love. And he'd been distracted enough to lose the pattern of the car as it started to shake. He would just do it one more time. "Let's find out about that shimmy and bring in New Year's with a bang," he said.

The motor caught and the deep throb of its power vibrated through the car with its sloped nose and high back that was reminiscent of a rocket in design. Then Brokaw hit the doorframe with one hand and stood back.

"Okay, it's a go. One more time. But watch the wheel."

Coop slipped the car into gear, and with a thumbs-up sign, he eased back onto the track. *Nothing to lose.* The words echoed in him, and the memory of when he'd told Dylan the same thing came right along with it. He built up speed, but even amid the arid Spanish countryside that surrounded the test area, he couldn't block the memories of the rain and Dylan.

He pressed the accelerator more, talking into the mouthpiece to record the speed and rpms and the car's responses. But his thoughts were in the past and on the future. January. In two days he could be out of here and going back. And for the first time since he'd been a teenager, he was getting impatient to see a girl. There had been a lot of women in his life before—intelligent, beautiful, stirring women. But when he met Dylan, it was as if those women had never existed.

Right then he knew what it was to be afraid, to think of never seeing Dylan again, of doing one thing that could destroy a future. He'd barely formed the thought when it became a reality.

The car shuddered in the back. "Instability in the back end," he said as he approached the turn high. He eased back on the accelerator and hit the brakes. Then all hell broke loose. The pedal vibrated wickedly, echoing the shaking in the car itself, then it went right to the floor—but the car didn't slow.

"Brake failure with lateral movement," he said as he fought to right the wheel and go higher to make the turn. But as he forced the wheel to the left, he knew it was too late. The car started to rock, and when the safety wall came rushing at him, he knew with painful clarity that Brokaw had been so wrong.

He did have something to lose.

There were sparks of metal on cement, then the ripping of the car body. In seconds the car flipped in the air, and in a moment that felt like an eternity, the brilliant image of Dylan was with him, along with the agonizing regret that he had ever left her.

He'd lost everything.

DID THE DEAD DREAM?

Coop thought he must be dead. He knew something had happened that had cut him off from reality, and he was gradually falling into a place of blackness where nothing was real. He'd died. Oddly, he knew that must be what had happened, yet he was having a dream, and he was watching it unfold from the shadows.

He felt odd, disassociated; as if what was materializing was more a memory than a product of dreaming. But he could see Dylan, her image floating toward him out of the darkness. She was light and beauty, a focal point in a place that was blurred and unrecognizable. If he inhaled, he was certain he would be filled with her essence. If he reached out, he knew he could touch her, feel the silkiness of her skin under his finger and be able to feel the pulse beating wildly at the base of her throat.

His body tightened, and anything was possible. He could slip back into the past, watching her in the rain, touching her in the shadows of the bedroom. He could see her lips open with invitation, and see her hair falling free of the restraining knot to rest softly around her naked shoulders. He could take her, and reality could be blotted out for a heartbeat or for an eternity. And he could stay there forever.

But even as that thought materialized, he knew it was wrong. Even though she was close, he couldn't do anything. He wanted to take a breath and absorb her essence, but he couldn't. His lungs were tight and unresponsive. Need overwhelmed him. He tried to reach out, but he couldn't move.

He tried to say her name, but his throat closed and words wouldn't come. She began to dissolve into the darkness, a shimmering image that was being lost to him. Then suddenly he was in a car, the Mercedes, and he could see Dylan in the BMW ahead of him, coming at him. Rain was everywhere, brakes squealed and the smell of burned rubber filled the air.

He wanted to scream for her to stop as the BMW hurled toward him, but he couldn't scream. He couldn't press the brakes or turn the wheel, and he knew that impact was a certainty. But it never came.

In that moment, he was jerked out of the darkness and he knew he wasn't dead. He was awake. Death wouldn't hurt this much.

It didn't take any time for him to know where he was. He was in the hospital, and he remembered the accident, and in a flash that made him flinch inwardly, he remembered the impact. His last thought— the thoughts that had brought the nightmares now— haunted him.

He'd survived. But he didn't know what the cost of that survival would be. Not until the doctor got here to give him the results of the last barrage of tests they'd done earlier. One thing he knew, if he got a green light, as soon as he could he was flying out of here and back to San Diego. All he wanted was to see Dylan again.

A door clicked open somewhere to his right, jerking him back to the present, and he heard footsteps on the hard floor tiles. The clicking came closer, and he could almost feel someone staring down at him. Then a hand touched his shoulder. But the voice didn't belong to his doctor.

"Coop, hey, Coop." Brokaw spoke in a low, urgent voice. "Are you awake?"

He eased his eyes open to a dull glow somewhere to the left. Then he could see Brokaw hovering over him in the shadows.

"I thought you were awake," Brokaw said.

"Where's the doctor?"

"He'll be here in a few minutes, but I thought I should talk to you first."

Coop could feel something else coming, something that Brokaw was uneasy about. "Why?"

"I thought it was a good idea." He studied Coop, then took a deep breath. "Hey, you took a licking, and you're still ticking."

"Why don't you just tell me what they sent you in to tell me."

Brokaw moved back a bit more into the shadows. "You took a hard hit. You know that. You know there's bruising around your ribs and heart, and your legs... They're fractured."

"Tell me something I don't know."

Brokaw hesitated before continuing, "The doctor can explain it in detail to you, but in layman's terms, it's worse than they thought." He paused, as if to give Coop time to react. But he didn't. He just kept staring at Brokaw. "Okay, the fractures in both legs are multiple, and in your right leg, there's extensive nerve damage."

"Get to the bottom line."

"They have to operate again, insert pins in both legs to hold the bones in place and see if they fuse properly. And the nerves... There's no way to know if they'll rejuvenate or not."

He sank back and closed his eyes. "So, I might not walk again, is that it?"

"No. They're hopeful things will go well, but there's a chance you won't get full use of your legs."

"How long before they know?" he demanded.

"There's no timetable for it. But within a year they'll probably know the extent of the irreversible damage."

Coop had dealt with a lot of painful things in his life, but this was beyond pain. It literally took the ability out of him to feel anything except a grief that made little sense. "Irreversible damage?"

"Hey, don't borrow trouble. Wait and see what happens, and don't worry about your job. Your contract's good for the five years, working or not, so you're covered."

"Swell," he muttered.

"I'll go and get the doctor."

Coop took two deep breaths, then opened his eyes to face the man standing over him. "Tell the doctor to wait. I need to make a phone call."

Brokaw moved, then held out a phone receiver for him. "What's the number?"

Coop gave the number to him from memory, then held the cold receiver to his ear. He heard the call going through, and paid no attention to Brokaw leaving the room. After three rings, there was a click, then he heard Dylan on the other end of the line.

"Hello?"

He literally flinched at the sound of her voice, so clear she might have been in the next room. He closed his eyes so tightly that he saw colors burst behind his eyelids.

"Hello, is anyone there?" she asked.

He hadn't known what he was thinking when he put in the call. Had he thought he could tell her he was detained, and that he would be back in a while? Or had he thought he would tell her what had happened and have her drop her life in San Diego to come over here to be with an invalid? None of that made sense.

Now he knew what real pain was. He wouldn't be going back. He couldn't go back like this. He wouldn't. Not until he could walk. If he ever could again. And he couldn't listen to her voice. He twisted, trying to put the phone back in the cradle, but the receiver slipped from his fingers and clattered to the hard floor.

He sank back into the pillows, a film of perspiration on his face from the exertion, and he heard her one last time, a faint voice in the distance.

"Hello, hello?" Then it was gone, and a dial tone droned from the earpiece on the floor.

Chapter Nine

San Diego
Fourth of July

"Hot, hot, hot," the voice on the radio was saying. "San Diego is shaking and baking on this holiday. Heat in excess of one hundred degrees is blanketing the city and even the beach is boiling at ninety-nine. Up and down the West Coast, temperatures are setting records, from Seattle to the Mexican border and into the neighboring states. And there's no relief in sight. Public utilities are urging everyone to take it easy on the air-conditioning and reduce the load on the power supplies."

When the doorbell rang, Dylan flipped off the radio in the kitchen and left the lemonade she was making on the sink to go and answer the door. Despite the assorted fans she had around the house, nothing was making her feel cooler, and by the time she got to the door, the gauzy sundress she wore was sticking to her skin.

As she reached for the door, whoever was out there kicked the wooden barrier. "Dylan, it's me," she heard Tori call, in one look out the side window she spotted Tori's white van sitting by the curb. She grabbed the handle and pulled back the barrier. "Tori, what's going—"

Tori had her arms full of boxes and didn't wait for an invitation before coming into the house. Dylan moved back to let her pass as her sister called out, "Happy, happy birthday!"

Dylan swung the door shut and turned to see Tori dropping the boxes on the couch by the hearth. "Thanks," she murmured.

Tori turned, looking flushed and hot in white shorts and a pink halter top. "Boy, it's like an oven in here. I told you you should have had air-conditioning installed. Allan could have done it for you."

Dylan leaned back against the door. "What's going on? I thought I was supposed to be coming to your house for cake and fireworks later on."

"And you are, dear sister, but I had some things I wanted to bring by." She eyed Dylan. "Love your hair."

Dylan brushed a hand over her short cut, a blunt bob that exposed her neck and feathered at her bangs. "I thought it would help in this heat." She looked at the brown boxes on the couch. "You shouldn't have. But turning thirty doesn't happen every day, does it?"

"Oh, these aren't for you, at least not directly." She bent and grabbed the nearest box, took off the lid, then turned and held out a yellow sleeper that looked small enough to fit a doll. "They're for the baby, sweetie. Clothes and diapers and things. You know, the things you're supposed to buy."

Dylan brushed at her hair, not yet used to having it short. She turned from Tori. "Thanks," she murmured, and headed for the kitchen.

Tori wasn't far behind. "Hey, sometime or other, you have to do these things."

Dylan barely glanced at her enlarged stomach and crossed to the sink to finish the lemonade. She grabbed a knife, cut a lemon in half, then proceeded to juice it into a pitcher on the counter. "Things?"

"You know, clothes and blankets and cleaning out that second bedroom to make a nursery."

Dylan cut another lemon, juicing it with a vengeance. "I will. I just haven't—"

"Had the time . . . or the inclination."

Dylan dropped the knife with a clatter, then turned and leaned back against the counter. The house had been hot before, but now it was downright claustrophobic. She glanced at the sleeper in Tori's hands. "Thanks for the things."

"You're welcome. Oh, the natural childbirth classes, I checked into them and—"

"Tori, stop. It's too hot for this right now." She blew air upward to try and cool her forehead a bit. "I'll take care of things. Don't you worry about it."

"But you aren't."

"That's it. I don't need this lecture today. Things are...stressful right now. And I've got a million things to do." She looked down at the pitcher of lemonade, her stomach suddenly revolting at the idea of drinking it. What she needed was some sparkling water.

"Of course," Tori replied.

Dylan looked up at her. "What does that mean?"

"Cooper Reeves never came back. You never contacted him—"

"I didn't have his phone number or address."

"You had that Mr. Brokaw's number and address. You sent him enough money for that car."

"I told you, there was no point in contacting Coop."

"How would you know if—"

"Tori, stop it. I do know."

What Dylan hadn't known was what she'd expected when Coop came back in January, when he'd found out about the child. She hadn't known how he would react—if he would walk away, if he would be angry, or just not believe it was his—but she'd had no dreams that he would embrace the idea of a child with joy. Not any more than she had at first.

And she knew he would never understand her decision to have the child. There was no way she could have explained it to him when she didn't understand it herself. But she hadn't had to. He had never come back in January, and had never called again, so she'd been on her own.

She'd survived, and adjusted, and the pregnancy was a minor inconvenience at the moment. She was healthy as a horse, with no problems, and there were times, until the baby moved, when she had even forgotten she was pregnant. Until Tori started on her lectures about motherhood.

"I told you before, it's not your problem. It's mine. And I'll handle it."

"By ignoring it?"

She glanced down at her stomach. "How can I ignore it when I feel as if I'm being blown up like a hot air balloon."

"That's not true. You're not that big, not for almost eight months along. Heavens, when I was eight months with A.J.—"

"You were as big as an elephant."

"Thanks a lot."

"You're welcome. Now, I've got things to do."

"Dylan, have you heard the word *denial?*"

"Of course."

"Well, guess what? If you looked it up in the dictionary, you'd find your picture right by it."

That was it. She felt as if the walls were closing in on her and she was trapped in here with a sister who never stopped talking about children and pregnancy. She wanted out, and she grabbed at an excuse. "You should have called before coming over. I was just leaving."

"What about your lemonade?"

She picked up a glass, went to put ice in it, then poured lemonade into it and handed it to Tori. "Here. Enjoy. I'm out of here."

"Where are you going?" she asked, taking the drink. "Oh, no, you don't have to tell me. You're going down to those buildings, aren't you?"

She hadn't thought she was, not then, but suddenly she knew she was going to the Santa Clare buildings. She needed to. "Yes, I am."

"Why go out in this heat?"

She couldn't answer that with anything Tori would understand, so she lied. "The new car has great air-conditioning, and I've got some time, so I'll go to check on the moldings they put in yesterday."

"Oh, come on, Dylan, why now?"

"Why not? They've got the air-conditioning up and working this weekend to test it. It's going to be cool." She felt like a prisoner making her escape from the warden. "Lock up after yourself." She grabbed her purse, put her cell phone in it, and headed for the front door. "I'll see you for cake around eight, and if I'm going to be late, I'll call you."

"Dylan!" Tori called. "You're pregnant and you—" The words were thankfully cut off when Dylan closed the door behind her.

Dusk was just starting to fall on the city, and the heat outside was like a furnace. As Dylan crossed to the new car she'd just managed to buy to replace her old BMW, she blocked out Tori's words. She didn't want to be reminded of being pregnant, or reminded of Coop. Not now.

She got into her dark blue car with tinted windows and as soon as she started it, the air-conditioning kicked in. Welcome coolness brushed her bare arms right away. As she slipped the car into reverse, she saw the front door open and Tori come hurrying out. She was holding the lemonade in one hand and waving at Dylan with the other.

Dylan almost stopped, but instead ignored the sight and backed out the driveway, then drove off down the street without looking into the rearview mirror. At the stop sign, she turned to the right and drove off toward the freeway.

She neared the on-ramp and spotted a convenience store that was all new, all glass and spread out on a corner that had once been occupied by a small market that had been part of the neighborhood until development took over. She hated the way it looked right there, but it sold cold sparkling water, and she really was thirsty.

Just as she pulled into the parking lot, a black Porsche roared past, going in the opposite direction. Dylan drove by the gas pumps and around to the side to park. As she went into the store, she knew she'd been lying to Tori about going to the buildings, but when she waited for what seemed an interminable amount of time in the line to pay for her drink and apple, she decided that she really would go.

No one was there but the security guard, and she would have the space all to herself. More important, she would have time to figure out how to close whatever gap was still in her life from Coop walking away from her.

She was third in line and impatient to get on with things. Perhaps making one last visit to the building was the only way she could put an end to that part of her life. And maybe it would be the only way she could come to terms with her new life—a new life that would include a child who deserved more than a mother who was haunted by the past.

"COOP, I TOLD YOU, I've checked with the firm you asked me to contact, and they said she quit." Brokaw drove his black Porsche off the freeway and onto the dusky evening streets leading toward Dylan's house. "They said she got a private contract and as far as they know, she's working on it. The woman said something about her saying she had big changes in her professional and private lives to deal with, and that's all she knew. Apparently her bosses weren't too thrilled with what she was doing. My guess is they wanted the job she got."

"You already told me that," Coop muttered and pointed ahead of them to the turn for Dylan's street. "Just take a right up there. Her house is near the end."

"What if she's not there?" Brokaw asked.

Coop stared ahead from the passenger seat of the black Porsche Brokaw had purchased to replace the Mercedes. "I don't know. I just wish I could remember her sister's last name."

"What's the deal?" Brokaw demanded. "First you didn't want any part of San Diego. You insisted on staying in Spain. Then, all of a sudden, you had to come back and find the maniac driver who smashed up my car. Why now?"

Maniac driver? He would have smiled at that description of Dylan if he hadn't been so nervous and edgy. He rubbed at his right thigh through the cotton beige slacks he was wearing with a white, open-necked shirt that was already sticking to his skin. The ache in his bad leg was constant, and was aggravated by getting in and out of the low-slung car. But it seemed just a minor nuisance at the moment.

He pressed his palm against his thigh and exhaled on a hiss. "Yesterday I found out that things are going well, and there isn't a chance of losing my leg."

"I know. You told me already. What does that have to do with this mad search for Dylan Bradford?"

"I was going to come back to see her in January, but the accident short-circuited my plans. But now that things have worked out, I wanted to see her again."

"I knew there was more to this search than just looking up someone who ran into you."

Coop chuckled at that. "She ran into me, all right."

"But . . . ?"

"Okay, I like her. We had a good time, and I couldn't forget about her." While he'd gone through two operations and interminable physical therapy, and had lived under the threat of possibly losing his right leg, his refuge had been in his dreams of Dylan. His memories of her could soothe long hours of pain. "I just want to see her," he said with aching truthfulness.

"So you flew all the way from Spain with a leg that must hurt like hell with all those pins in it, just because you wanted to see her?"

"Yeah, but I never thought I wouldn't be able to find her. That her phone would ring and ring without an answer."

Brokaw turned onto Dylan's street, and Coop found himself sitting forward in his seat to spot the house. "There," he said as a white van drove past them in the opposite direction. "The one with the courtyard."

Brokaw neared the house, then pulled into the driveway. Before the car had come to a full stop, Coop had the door open. "Wait right here," he said, levering himself out of the car as quickly as he could.

The heat hit him full force, but he hardly noticed it any more than he noticed the discomfort in his bad leg now. He went around the Porsche to the courtyard gate and pushed back the warm metal barrier. He could feel his heart starting to pound, and he found himself actually slowing as he neared her front door. What could he say to her? How could he explain the fiasco in January?

He stopped by the door and prayed that she would even talk to him, let alone let him explain why he'd stood her up. He knocked on the wood, but there was no response. He knocked again, and when nothing happened, he moved back a bit. He could see a light on somewhere in the house, but there was no movement, no sound. The house felt empty.

He moved farther back and almost walked into a small metal table under the olive tree. He turned and saw a glass sitting on the patterned metal, and he reached for it. It was damp and cold to his touch. When he picked it up and sniffed it, he could smell the pungency of lemonade. Ice cubes floated in the beverage. Someone had to have been here only minutes ago.

He put the glass down, went back and knocked on the door again. Still nothing happened. "Damn it all," he muttered as he limped back through the courtyard and out to the Porsche. As he got into the car, he said, "No one's home."

Brokaw started the engine and eased back onto the street. "Maybe she doesn't live there anymore. Maybe she's moved or left town. Maybe her new job was out of town, and not around here."

"Thanks for the encouragement," Coop retorted as Brokaw's words made his stomach churn. "Any more words of cheer?"

"I need gas."

Coop glanced up the street toward the freeway and saw a gas-station and convenience-store combination. "You're in luck," he said, motioning toward the complex on the corner near the on-ramp.

Brokaw pulled into the parking lot, stopped by the pumps, and started to sort through his wallet for a credit card. He was taking forever, and Coop finally said, "I'll get it," and opened his door. "Fill it up. I'll go inside and pay for it."

"Hey, you don't have to—"

"I do, if I ever want to get out of here," he said with exasperation, then got out of the car, grabbed his cane and headed for the store area and the cashier.

He stepped into the glass-paned structure and got into a line with maybe a dozen people in it. He pulled money out of his pocket, then looked ahead at the cashier and took a deep breath. In that moment, he felt his heart lurch. The scent in the air, just the hint of a certain fragrance, caught at him with shocking force. It was the same perfume that Dylan wore. The one he remembered. The one he could close his eyes and imagine so easily.

He looked around, then saw a dark-haired woman just going out the door. With a motion that cost him a great deal of pain, he pivoted and hurried after her. He grabbed the door that was just closing, jerked it open and went outside. He saw the woman stop for a dark blue car as it passed her on its way to the street, then she turned and he caught a glimpse of her profile.

He'd been a fool. She wasn't Dylan, wasn't even close to the reality. It was all an illusion caused by that phantom scent in the store, by dark hair that curled softly around slim shoulders, and an aching need in him to see Dylan again.

"Damn it all," Coop muttered, holding tightly to the cane to take some of the pressure off his bad leg. Then he turned and, favoring his sore leg, he slowly went back inside to pay for Brokaw's gas.

As DYLAN DROVE ONTO the street where the Santa Clare buildings were, she saw a transformed area. Graffiti were gone, the trash was a thing of the past, and the buildings looked clean. The exteriors were almost finished, and the walkways had been widened to include tree cutouts near the curbs next to the gas lamps.

She pulled in to the curb to park beside a gas lamp and tree, but she didn't get out immediately. She had an impulse to just drive off, but she couldn't. She had to do this, and do it now. "Happy birthday to me," she muttered, then dropped her keys in her purse and got out into the sweltering heat of early evening.

She walked slowly around the car, thankful her dress was light, with narrow straps and a long, loose skirt that brushed her bare legs. By the time she reached the entry doors, her skin was sleek with moisture and her newly shorn hair was sticking to her neck and forehead.

She pushed back the doors and stepped into the completely renovated lobby. The marble floor gleamed, the round desk was buffed to perfection, and the walls were completely redone in rough plaster. Thankfully, the air-conditioning was going full force. The cool breeze caressed her naked arms and she exhaled deeply.

"Sure feels good, don't it, Ms. Bradford?"

She turned to her right and saw the night guard, Chuck, an imposing-looking man with dark hair and an immaculate gray uniform. He stood behind the security desk, his hat pushed back on his head. He'd been posted here since last week when they'd started using the front entry instead of the construction entrance from the underground parking area.

"It feels great." She sighed. "Wonderful."

"It's been working real good. Only a few surges."

"That's good," she replied and glanced at the elevators. The framed print she'd donated to the building had been hung here just a few days ago—the print of the original view of the building by Winston Lee.

"That Mr. Dytmyer says they're going to have some ceremony soon for the opening," Chuck said.

"They're having a black-tie reception here on August the first for the grand opening."

He smiled at her as she glanced back at him. "And when's the other big day for you?"

She touched her middle through the light gauze material, always surprised by the fullness of her stomach even though Tori pointed it out every chance she got. Then the baby shifted slowly, rolling from one side to the other, and she pulled her hand back quickly. "August eighth."

"Whoa!" he said with a grin. "You planned all this down to the minute, didn't you?"

She swallowed hard and couldn't smile at his words. Her timing had been anything but good. She turned and headed across to the elevators. "I just hope it all works out," she replied in a voice that was slightly tight.

As she paused to hit the Up button, she saw herself in the polished brass doors. She looked so different from that night she'd come here with Coop, and it wasn't just the short hair. The other woman was long gone, and in her place was a sober-faced pregnant woman who couldn't remember the last time she'd laughed.

"I'm going on my rounds in a bit. If I'm not here when you come down, just make sure the doors close tightly behind you," Chuck called to her. "Sometimes they don't click all the way."

Dylan pushed the button for the fourteenth floor and nodded to the man across the room. "I'll make sure I do."

"Oh, by the way, is it a boy or a girl?"

"I don't know," she called back as the doors silently slid shut.

As the car started smoothly upward, she had a momentary flashback to the time with Coop, when the car had stopped between floors. And the panic in her was so real that she had to force herself to stay very still and take deep breaths. It was the past—just a memory, not reality anymore. And she needed to be rid of it. She needed that with a desperation she knew had been building until this moment.

When the doors opened, she stepped quickly into the refurbished reception rotunda, and in the soft light of wall sconces, the memories crowded in again. They didn't stop. She closed her eyes tightly for a moment and tried to ignore the baby slowly moving to reposition itself. Coop was gone. He'd left, and it couldn't be more simple. No more simple than the fact that at that moment, she hated him.

Quickly she opened her eyes, then turned and started down the hallway lit by side fixtures recessed in the paneling. Each step she took toward the farthest office reinforced the idea that she was here to say goodbye.

She pushed back the newly refinished walnut doors, then entered the reception space of the buildings most expensive office. She flipped on the overhead lights, and the glow flooded a large, open area where two walls had been removed. Off-white carpeting, antique brass fixtures and a built-in marble-topped desk facing the doors gave a feeling of expansive elegance. She crossed to the executive office and went in through the open door.

Here, there were no lights on, but the windows were bare. The coming night and the glow from city lights invaded the area and the only sound was the low hiss of the air-conditioning unit. As the door started to swing shut, she caught it with one hand and pushed it back against the wall to keep it open. She didn't want to be closed in here. Not in this room.

Quickly, she flipped on the lights, exposing some furniture that the new tenant had already brought in. There were two tweed barrel chairs over near the windows and a long, narrow table along the far wall. Built-in bookshelves to the right were high enough to reach the domed ceiling.

She stood very still, then knew she didn't want light. She wanted shadows and gentleness around her. Reaching to her right, she flipped the switch, shutting off the soft glow, and moved silently to the windows. It was a spectacular sight, where stars and a partial moon shimmered through the still, hot air. Lights dotted the land around the bay, and a few fireworks were being set off to the south near Coronado.

She laid her purse on the nearest chair, then unlatched the window in front of her. It opened effortlessly now, letting in a wave of heat, but it was worth it to be able to inhale the scent of the nearby ocean and to hear the sounds of traffic below.

As she ran one finger along the unfinished metal edging on the glass, her hand jerked when music started in the distance. It was from the fifties club, a rendition of "Blue Moon," and it came up to her clearly on the hot air.

She slowly drew her hand back as the memory of "You Send Me" overlapped the present—a memory of music drifting through a rainy night to the same deserted office, and of dancing with a stranger. But now there was heat and newness—and no man holding her and moving slowly to the gentle music.

She shook her head sharply to get past the memories, and yet, for a flashing moment, she felt such longing for the past that it all but choked her. She'd been right to decide not to come back here again after the job was done. She had to get on with her life—a life that didn't include Cooper Reeves or memories of him that could haunt her in this place. She knew it was over—once and for all. She had to get on with her life alone.

But then she felt the baby kick, and in a startling moment when she felt she had nothing left, she realized how wrong she'd been. The baby. This new life inside her. Her child. And suddenly she connected with the child in a way she would never have believed she could; in a way she hadn't allowed herself to before now. She hadn't even wanted Dr. Barnette to tell her if it was a boy or a girl.

But now she knew she wasn't alone at all. She had the child—a child that would count on her for everything in its life for a very long time. And the barriers fell. She didn't know how it happened, but she could literally feel herself sensing everything about the baby.

There was a closure within her, a moment in time when she understood and accepted what was happening to her. Coop was thousands of miles away, living the life he wanted to live. Even though she'd thought she hated him, she didn't. She couldn't. But she could let go of him. And now, in the silent office, she finally did.

Chapter Ten

"The restaurant is less than ten minutes from here, so what do you say we go to the party, see the fireworks, then I'll drive you all over the city if you want?"

Coop slouched in the low-slung seat and stared out at the city, at the night sky and heat lightning that cut through the heavens. "I should have stayed at her house and waited for someone to come back."

"As I said, if she still lives there," Brokaw reminded with annoying logic.

"Just take me back there."

Brokaw glanced at his wristwatch. "Can't it wait for a while? We won't be at the party more than a few hours, just long enough for the fireworks and some drinks. Hey, you've been gone eight months, so another few hours won't make any difference, will they?"

Eight months. A long time. A lifetime. And Coop hated to wait even another minute. He wanted to see if what he remembered was real or just an illusion that had been with him for so long he mistook it for reality. An illusion like the times he'd been thrown off when he'd see a woman with long dark hair walking in the rain, or when it was a cool, misty night and a slender woman came toward him from the shadows. Or when he'd heard rain and music and thought of dancing in the old offices.

Then Coop knew one more place to try, the place where it had all begun for him. He shifted in the seat to ease the ache in his leg as he said, "There is a place that's around here somewhere. The Santa Clare buildings. Do you know where they are?"

"Sure. I think they're just up there," Brokaw replied, motioning ahead of them.

Coop looked up and saw a familiar turn. "Yes, that's it," he said, thankful that something was working out with relative ease.

As they turned onto the street, heat lightning ripped across the sky and he blinked as the pale light exposed the past, but a transformed past. The whole area had the ambience of a European street, with exposed brick and stone on the facades. There were cobbled walkways, newly refurbished exteriors of upscale business buildings, and trees set with gas lamps by the curb.

"Is this the place?" Brokaw asked.

"Yes," he breathed at the same moment he saw a car parked in front of the main building. A dark blue sedan. A car that looked like Dylan's BMW parked right where they had when they'd come here eight months ago.

"Stop the car," Coop said abruptly. "Park over there behind that car. That's her car. The one she hit the Mercedes with."

"Why would she be parked down here?"

He wasn't about to explain about the buildings. He didn't have time to do that. "She knows the area," he said quickly. "Just park."

"I thought you said she drove a BMW?"

Coop blinked, and knew how wrong he'd been, just about as wrong as he'd been in the convenience store. "She does. She did."

"For someone who knows cars, you're pretty short on this one. That's a Ford, isn't it?"

He nodded. "I guess so."

"Do you still want me to stop?" he asked as he slowed even more.

Coop looked up at the buildings, then said, "Yes." He didn't want to go to a party, or go to see fireworks. Right now he wanted to see an old building that someone had cared enough about, to restore to its former glory. "Just let me out here."

Brokaw glanced at his watch as he slowed the car and swung toward the curb. "We don't have much time, so—"

"You don't have to wait. Go on to the party."

"But that's not her car."

"No, it's not, but don't worry about me. I'll find my own way to the party."

"But it's an oven out there."

"Just give me the address of the restaurant."

Brokaw pulled in behind the sedan. "Are you sure about this?"

"Absolutely," he said as he flipped open the door and grabbed his cane, then carefully maneuvered himself out of the low car onto the cobbled walkway. He could feel his skin filming with moisture, and when he managed to get onto his feet, his leg was really throbbing.

"The restaurant's two blocks up, then right. The Atrium," Brokaw said as he leaned across the passenger seat to look up at Coop.

Coop nodded. "Got it. See you later," he said and swung the door shut.

Brokaw revved the engine and took off, leaving Coop standing on the sidewalk taking hot air into his lungs and leaning heavily on his cane. He looked around and despite the changes, that rainy October evening came back with a vividness that made him grip the cane tightly. He turned and started for the entrance of the main building.

It didn't look as if it was open yet, but one door was slightly ajar. When he tugged it open, a wave of coolness spilled out at him. He stepped into the softly lit interior, where the transformation was as complete as outside.

He looked around, didn't see anyone, then crossed to the elevators on the back wall. As he approached the doors, he hesitated. The print he'd seen at Dylan's house, her prized Winston Lee print, the line drawing of this building, hung on the wall by the elevator doors.

He slowly approached the elevators, then glanced up at the floor indicators and saw that one of them was stopped on the fourteenth floor. The top floor. The best offices in the building. Unique offices. And he knew he was going up to see them one last time.

DYLAN STOOD BY THE windows, feeling as if a weight had been lifted off her shoulders. She actually smiled when the baby kicked just under her ribs. Looking down, she shocked herself when she touched her stomach and spoke to her child for the first time.

"Okay, I know you're there," she murmured, feeling slightly awkward and embarrassed to be talking to her stomach.

As heat lightning cut through the night, casting a pale glow over the city below, the baby kicked again. "I know, I hate lightning, too. But if I were you, I'd be relaxing and taking advantage of the free ride while you can." She sighed and shifted her hand to her back to press against a dull ache that had just begun there. "Trust me, kid, when you get out into this world, you'll realize how good you have it now."

Another kick got her ribs. "Okay, no lectures," she said with a soft chuckle. "I won't go that far. But since we're here alone, I think there're a couple of things we should get straight.

"I guess you know by now it's going to be just the two of us. And to be honest with you, I'm not sure I'm going to be a very good mother."

She looked down at her stomach again and marveled at how right it felt to be here with her child. Tori would be astonished if she knew that her sister was actually feeling maternal. But that didn't mean she would know what to do, or how to do it. "Listen, give me a break, and don't be too jealous of A.J. when Aunt Tori bakes him brownies and knits him socks and makes his Halloween costume from her old drapes."

She glanced back out at the city, then off into the distance beyond the bay. "I'm afraid it's probably fast food and bare feet for us, kiddo. And you'll have to be patient until I get the hang of this parenting thing, because I wasn't born to it like your Aunt Tori. Not even close."

When the baby stayed still, she sighed. "I'm glad you understand that." She touched the edge of the open window. "Now, you're never too young to learn. When you're in charge of your own business, you have to keep on top of things. You need to check and double-check, and when you do a job, do it right. Be proud of it. I'm proud of this place. But I'm not coming back when it's done. I'll move on, get another contract, and you're going to have to get used to being in and out of old buildings."

The baby kicked her sharply in the side, then rolled and settled low in the front. "Okay, maybe you won't have to go at first. Aunt Tori would be glad to have you entertain A.J." She shifted her hand to pat her stomach, wondering if she was patting a bottom or a head. "Right now, it's my birthday, and Aunt Tori has cake for us."

Without warning, the lights flickered behind her— once, twice—then stayed on. With a sigh, she said, "It's okay. Let's just relax for a minute and enjoy one last look at this view. Just one more moment, then we'll go and have some birthday cake with A.J. and Aunt Tori and Uncle Allan."

She exhaled softly, then, as she made slow circles on her stomach with the tips of her fingers, she started to hum the song coming up from the club, "Be My Baby." When lightning flashed again, she closed her eyes and for the first time since she'd found out she was pregnant, she wished she knew whether the baby was a boy or a girl.

Coop was certain he was losing it when he got on the elevator and thought again that he caught a hint of the perfume Dylan wore. "Crazy," he muttered, but made very sure he didn't breathe too deeply until the elevator stopped at the fourteenth floor and the doors opened.

He slowly got out, but something made him reach back and hold the elevator doors open. Maybe this wasn't such a good idea. Maybe it was a form of masochism. And maybe he should leave. He could take a taxi back to the house and wait. And if she never came, he would leave.

His stomach knotted, but he knew that there wasn't anything else to do. He glanced around the rotunda area, then turned to get back on the elevator. That was when he spotted the open doors at the end of the hallway and the hint of light spilling out into the softly lit corridor.

When he would have started toward the doors, the lights suddenly flickered a couple of times within a matter of seconds, then burned steadily. Slowly he let go of the elevator doors and as they slid shut, he knew he couldn't leave just yet. He turned and started down the corridor toward the light, the sound of his cane muffled on the expensive carpeting.

When he got to the doors and stepped inside, he glanced around, then caught that scent again—light, airy and "Dylan." He almost held his breath, but cautiously took another breath. Yes, he wasn't imagining it. It was real. And the door to the inner office was open.

He silently crossed the thick, deep carpeting, then stopped at the open door. Slowly he leaned the cane against the wall and gripped the doorframe on either side. Through the shadows, beyond a pair of low chairs, he saw a silhouette in front of the windows, a slender woman framed against the night.

She looked as if she was almost part of that night. Soft folds of a sleeveless dress floated around her hips and partway down her calves. Her hair looked as if it had been pulled back to expose the sweep of her throat, and she stood very still. The woman looked like Dylan.

If he was mad, so be it. This madness had produced Dylan, had given him what he'd wanted for what seemed a lifetime. Another bolt of lightning cut through the night. The pale light bathed her bare shoulders, touched her hair, and for a flashing moment, showed the silhouette of long, slender legs through the thin material. His reaction to her, whether she was real or an illusion, was as sudden and violent as the lightning that was fading away.

His madness went even further when he heard distant music drifting into the room. As the heat lightning criss-crossed the sky again, he knew the delusions came from the past, from that night with music and rain—the night they'd danced in this room.

It seemed so real. She seemed so real. Yet he couldn't let himself believe that she was here. He couldn't afford to let that madness become his reality. Then any question of his sanity was banished when she began to hum to the music with a soft, enticing sound that drew him like a moth to a flame. No apparition would sing old fifties songs.

It was Dylan.

He couldn't believe he'd found her. He wanted to rush to her and pull her close.

But he hesitated. He'd been gone months, and the best he hoped for was a second chance once he'd explained things. Just a second chance. That was all he could ask for. He took a slow, careful step toward her, bearing his weight on his bad leg, leaving his cane against the wall as he moved into the room. He didn't want her to see that—not until he could explain everything.

Advancing toward her, he ignored the discomfort in his leg as he eyes glided over her soft curves exposed by the filmy material of her dress. He stopped near the middle of the room and quietly said her name. "Dylan?"

The humming ended abruptly on a soft gasp, then slowly she looked back over her shoulder at him. A flash of lightning ripped the skies again, and as the white light exploded in the darkness, Coop felt a joy at seeing her that was almost painful. But the joy died with violent speed as she half turned to see who was there.

She was in profile, defined by the stark light for one heart-wrenching moment. He was no expert, but he didn't have to be one to see that she was pregnant.

As she stood very still in the fading light, even the shadows couldn't hide her state. She was pregnant not in the awkward, puffy way he would have expected in most women, but only with a gently swelling belly evident under the soft fabric of her sundress.

He swallowed hard at the sudden and shocking sense of loss that welled up in him when images bombarded him without warning. Brokaw had said something about "changes in her personal life." Changes?

The image of Dylan loving someone so much that she was doing something he never would have thought she would even consider, overwhelmed him. She was carrying that man's child.

And Coop knew that he never should have come back at all.

IT WAS A GHOST. An apparition in the shadows. For one crazy moment, Dylan thought it was Coop. She thought it was his voice, the set of his shoulders silhouetted by the lights of the outer office, his slightly shaggy hair. But it couldn't be.

This was a product of being alone in here at night, thinking about him, feeling his child moving and remembering and being haunted. She almost believed that, until lightning ripped through the night again and pale, eerie light flooded the room to expose the reality of Coop.

It etched his face in stark white and black—a face more gaunt than she remembered, a face with eyes lost in the darkness. And below it, a pale shirt open at the throat, strong arms exposed by short sleeves, and dark pants that molded to lean hips and long legs. The man she remembered, and a man she realized she would never let go. A part of her would always have been longing to see him one more time. The man standing there silently as the lightning faded, a dark silhouette with the light at his back and the emptiness of half the room between them.

Before she could do or say anything, Coop spoke in a voice that felt jarringly cool and distant—almost as if he were talking to a stranger and forcing himself to be polite. "Working on a holiday? Or were you just admiring what you've accomplished here?"

How could joy and fear be so perfectly mingled in her. She didn't know what to do to make sense of any of it. "A bit of both," she admitted.

"You've done a good job," he murmured, and she braced herself when he finally moved. But he didn't come over to her. Instead, he walked slowly toward the sidewalls, and she could see that he was limping slightly, as if favoring his right leg. He almost blended into the shadows as he reached out to touch the built-in bookshelves, and she heard him exhale. "Nice touch."

She didn't want his approval of what she'd done here, and she didn't want to be so aware of everything about him. "I thought you were in Spain," she finally managed to get past the tightness in her throat.

"I was until yesterday." He moved silently on the thick carpet, running his hand along the shelves until he was near the windows in the far corner. "I flew in today."

"You're a bit late," she said.

"What's that old saying? 'Better late than never'?" He walked closer to the windows and glanced at her. She could almost feel his gaze on her stomach, the narrowing of his eyes, a certain tension in his stance. But he didn't say a word about what was so obvious.

When she'd thought he would be back in January, she'd been nervous and worried. A baby. The last thing he wanted. But she'd steeled herself, ready to tell him, then watch him leave. She knew that was what he would have done, and she thought she could have dealt with it then.

But right now, she wasn't at all sure she could deal with anything to do with Coop. Certainly not this indifference; the pretending she didn't have a stomach as big as a beach ball. The tinge of maternal feeling she'd started to feel just moments ago was rapidly growing into a sense of protectiveness for the child.

"If you say so," she said.

"Things came up, and I couldn't get away."

A flash through the windows startled Dylan and she glanced at the evidence of a shower of fireworks burning out over the bay. Then another followed, lighting the sky with blues and reds in shimmering brilliance. But all the time she was aware of Coop in the room, and her foolish hope that if she stayed very still, didn't talk and didn't look at him, she would find out she was imagining the whole thing.

But she knew how foolish that thought was when he spoke from a place much closer to her. "A remarkable view, even without the rain."

She focused on the reflections in the glass, images of her with Coop less than three feet to her right. God, this was so crazy. Painfully polite talk when she really wanted to get this over with. "Yes," she murmured as she closed her eyes to the images in front of her.

"And I see you kept the windows so they opened," he said.

"It adds to the uniqueness, and it keeps with the past." God, she hated this patter. She hated it with a vengeance. "It doesn't violate it in any way."

There was a flash of light that she could sense with her eyes closed, then Coop said, "Fireworks. Happy Birthday."

He'd remembered, and she hated that, too. She didn't want him to be here remembering things about her. She made herself open her eyes and looked through the glass to the bay and the scattering of fireworks in the distance. Everyone had told her her thirtieth birthday would be hard, but she had never thought it could be this hard. And she wanted it over and done.

"Thanks."

She could feel him looking at her. Then he said, "You cut your hair."

And I'm very pregnant, she wanted to say, but instead asked in a voice she barely recognized as her own, "Why are you here now?"

"I was in the neighborhood, and saw the doors open. So I thought I'd come on in."

"No, that's not what I meant," she replied as she turned to him, hating the way her voice was beginning to shake.

He hesitated, then cast her a slanting glance that was almost her undoing. But she made herself keep looking at him, more than thankful for the relative darkness around them. "Then tell me what you meant."

She moved her shoulders in a fluttery, uncertain action that echoed the way she was feeling. "You said you'd be back in January, and you weren't. Then suddenly you show up here now." She hugged her arms around herself to try and steady her reactions. "Why?"

He turned toward her more and his eyes were hidden in the darkness. "Why not?"

She wasn't up to this. "Don't do this."

"Don't do what?"

"Don't play games."

"I wasn't aware this was a game."

"What is it, then?"

"I'd say two old friends were meeting again after a long absence and talking to each other. I don't see that as playing games. I just wanted to say hello, see how things were going for you and maybe finish up my tour of the city."

She swallowed hard as sickness started to rise in her throat when the past flooded over her. "Just like that?"

"Why not?"

If he wasn't going to say anything about the baby, she had to. "Isn't it obvious?"

She braced herself, knowing the moment had come when he would ask her about the child—about his child—and she just hoped she could do this and get through it.

But he was quiet for a very long time before he jarred her, saying, "I thought you said you didn't like kids. That a kid was the last thing you wanted."

"It was," she admitted.

"Then what's going on?"

"Obviously I'm pregnant."

The words hung between them, and she waited for the question that had to come. For the moment when she would tell him the child was his, and he would walk away.

She flinched when he muttered, "I'd say you don't need any more lessons on living for the moment."

The cutting edge of his words tore at her, and she found herself striking back. "Live for the moment, don't think about tomorrow. You remember the litany. Well, guess what, Coop? Tomorrow comes. And sometimes it isn't at all what we expect it to be. Surprise."

She knew just how far removed he was from even thinking the child could be his when he said, "Was it a surprise for the father, too?"

She knew this was the chance she was looking for, the time to tell him the truth and pick up the pieces, but something stopped her. That feeling of protectiveness for her baby grew to an intensity that she could barely comprehend. In that moment she realized that the child was the important thing here—not her, not her feelings, and not Coop.

That solidified her initial decision not to contact him about the pregnancy. He didn't need to know at all. He didn't want to know. He didn't want that problem in his life, and she wasn't going to force it on him. "A surprise for everyone," she replied.

Coop studied her intently, and she could hear him take each breath. "So, you got married?" he asked unexpectedly.

She knew she could get this all over with if she just lied, and said what he expected. That was the sensible thing to do, the thing that would stop all confrontations, all arguments, all recriminations. It would protect everyone.

She pressed her hand hard to her back, arching slightly and inadvertently making her pregnancy more evident in the process. Lies didn't come easily to her, but she made herself say, "Yes."

"You never mentioned anyone when we talked on the phone."

"And you didn't come back or call again, so we're even," she told him. "Now I have to take care of a few things before I leave. Tori's having a birthday party for me, and I'm running late."

Suddenly the lights flashed—once, twice, in a strange, all-encompassing burst of illumination. Then there was nothing.

She'd seen to it that the electrical wiring had been thoroughly checked out and updated during the renovation, and for a moment she thought the building would be a failure before it even opened. Then she looked out the windows and realized that the power failure wasn't just in this building. There were no lights anywhere in the city.

The sight of San Diego in total darkness was eerie, and scary. It was as if the world had disappeared in a flash, leaving only the moon and stars, a scattering of car lights, shimmering hot air, and the man beside her.

"What's happening?" she breathed.

"It looks like a massive power failure," Coop said, closer to her now.

She pressed a hand to the edge of the open window and flinched when she heard sirens in the distance, then car horns and a dull roar of people below. The music was gone. "But how? I mean, it's...it's all over the city," she said, watching cars snake through the streets.

"It's probably just temporary."

"What are we going to do?"

"I could sing the full *Gilligan's Island* theme song," he said. "Remember? I know all the words."

The joke jarred her and she muttered, "I wasn't talking about singing."

"Sorry." He didn't sound at all sorry for the poor attempt at humor.

A flash of heat lightning burst through the sky, illuminating the city below for a split second. Then it was gone and the darkness was all around again. When the baby kicked suddenly, low and hard, she gasped and pressed a hand to her stomach.

"Hey, are you all right?" Coop asked.

She glanced at him, and without lights, there was no way to read his expression. "The baby kicked," she said, and suddenly wished she could take his hand and hold it to her stomach so he could feel the life inside her. For one moment she wanted to share the wonder with him, but she knew that she was past that sort of fantasy. Long past it.

Chapter Eleven

Dylan clenched her hand into a fist on her stomach as Coop came even closer. Suddenly she felt very tired, and she sat down in the chair nearest to her. With a sigh she settled, but any relief was short-lived when Coop approached her, crouching in front of the chair. It echoed the positions they'd had at the hospital after the accident, and it made her very uncomfortable.

"You aren't close to having it, are you?" he asked.

She wasn't a liar, but it was getting easier for her to blur the truth. So she added a bit of time to her due date. "The baby's not due until September."

"Do you want me to call someone for you? Maybe your husband so he can come and get you?"

"No." The word was out before she could temper its abruptness. She held on to the arms of the chair tightly and tried to speak more easily. "I've got my car here."

"With this blackout—"

"You said it should be over soon. I'm actually going over to Tori's pretty soon."

He hesitated, then stood. He was going, and as soon as he left, she knew she could breathe again and try to relax. Maybe the ache in her back would let up. And maybe the relief she'd felt before he appeared would return to her.

But nothing with Coop went the way she thought it should. He stood over her, but instead of turning and walking away, he bent down again and shocked her when he touched her chin with two fingers. Gently he tipped her face up, and the contact points where his fingers touched her were almost painful for her.

"I'm not good at goodbyes," he whispered. "I hate them, even when I know I can't change them."

She bit her lip and swallowed hard. The memory of their last goodbye burned in her mind—the desperate loving, the need to hold and never let go. And she knew that was when she'd gotten pregnant. She didn't have any way to prove it, but she knew, somewhere deep inside. And that parting had been more painful than anything she'd done until January had come and gone without Coop coming back.

"You like to just fade off into the sunset, don't you?" she asked, her voice touched with a trace of bitterness she couldn't hide. "Just leave and not look back."

"I never intended to—" He cut off his own words, then said in a low voice, "I'm sorry I screwed things up, but some things just happen."

"Yes, they do," she said, knowing how true those words were. Her eyes were burning, and she made herself look up at Coop and say, "It's time for you to go, isn't it?"

"Yes, it is," he murmured, and she held her breath waiting for him to walk away. But he didn't leave then—he didn't stop the pain easily. He leaned toward her, placing a feathery kiss over her cold lips, and she closed her eyes tightly as she froze.

Then he drew back and she heard him whisper, "Have a good life, Dylan, and have a happy birthday."

Thankfully she didn't react the way she'd feared. When she opened her eyes, he was part of the shadows, a few feet away from her between the chair and the door to the outer office.

As he turned to go without another word, she pressed a hand to her mouth and closed her eyes again to shut out the sight of him heading for the door.

She knew that this time the leaving would be forever, with no promises to come back that he wouldn't keep. He wouldn't call. He wouldn't show up unexpectedly. He would ever touch her again. And he would never know that she had his child.

There was a soft click as the outer doors were closed, then the only sounds Dylan could hear were the city in distress far below. As she sat alone in the darkness, tears came. She hadn't cried since the last time Coop had left—not when she'd found out she was pregnant, and not when Coop hadn't come back. Now, though, silent tears ran down her cheeks and made her throat ache.

She rested one hand on her stomach as the baby stirred, and she opened her eyes. She swiped at the moisture on her cheeks and turned to the window and the darkness beyond. As more sirens wailed in the distance, she stroked her stomach and whispered unsteadily, "It's just you and me, kid."

As she released a tight breath, she tasted the saltiness on her lips. Then she swiped at her tears again. "And there's no more feeling sorry for ourselves. Okay? He's gone, but we'll do fine."

She took a deep, unsteady breath. "He's got his own life. And he's got to do what he needs to do. That just doesn't include us. He won't be back again, but that's not because of you, not really."

And words that had been deep inside her since the moment she'd known she was pregnant came out in a shaky whisper. "You know, I thought about lying to you when you got older and telling you he was dead. But I can't. So here's the truth. I only knew him for a little while, and he was gone before I even knew about you. Now he won't ever know about you. And that's for the best. I'm sure of it."

She swallowed hard. "I don't regret what happened with him or what my life is now." And that was the truth. Maybe it hadn't ended the way fairy tales did; maybe it left her hurt and more than a bit angry, and very pregnant. But she had her business, and she would have her child, and she would have a life. Not the one she'd planned, but one that she had to live.

As lightning ripped through the skies again, she whispered, "So, here I am, talking to my stomach and trying to figure out how to be a good mother." She took a deep breath again as the ache in her back made her a bit uncomfortable. "I promise to do the best I can, and if you'll give me a break from time to time, I'd appreciate it."

The child rolled slowly and gently, then settled softly. "Thanks, kid," Dylan breathed.

The sound of the outer door being opened startled her, before she realized the security guard was probably coming up to check on her. It really was time to go, to head over to her sister's, have her birthday cake and shock Tori when she told her that she wanted to start on the nursery tomorrow.

She turned to the door, saw the flash of a shadow there, then knew nothing was over when she heard Coop speak to her from the doorway. "You're going to have a hard time getting to your birthday party. The elevators are shut down and the stairwell doors are closed off. I came back to find out where the override for the system is."

"There isn't one."

He stayed by the door. "In a building like this, they don't have an override?"

"No, there is one, but it's not on-line. The system must have kicked on from the power failure."

"Then we're stuck here until the lights come back on, aren't we?" Coop said.

That idea was beyond endurance for her, and she gasped for some escape. She got up and reached for her purse on the other chair, then fumbled in it to get her cellular phone. She dropped the purse onto the floor by the chair. "I'll call the security guard and see if he can get the doors open from down there."

She flipped open the phone and a soft green glow from the keypad cast enough light for her to see that her finger was slightly unsteady as she pressed in the number for the front desk. "He's got a beeper with him all the time if a call comes through on the inside lines," she said as she pressed Send. There was a single ring, then a fast beeping sound. She knew that meant all the circuits were full.

She hit End and Coop asked, "Is there a problem?"

"It's not going through."

"Then I guess we have to wait this out."

The air was getting warm in the room since the air-conditioning had shut down, and her skin was already vaguely damp. She felt as if she couldn't quite take a full breath of air, and knew she didn't want to be here. "I'll try 911," she said and quickly pushed in the numbers. When she hit Send, it beeped, rang once, then went to a recording that started to give directions for any imaginable emergency, from fire to accidents.

She hit End and flipped the phone closed. A lot of people with real emergencies were calling—not people trapped in a hot room with a man who made it almost impossible for her to breathe, let alone think straight.

She jumped when Coop said, "No luck?" very close to her, and she quickly laid the phone on top of her purse. When she straightened, Coop was within a few feet of her.

"It's busy with real emergencies," she replied as she turned to the windows. She pressed the tips of her fingers to the warm glass and barely suppressed a shudder. Two separate fires flared into the skies on the far side of the bay. "My God, look at those fires over there. Why are there fires?"

"I don't know. Maybe people got careless with candles or maybe they don't have a thing to do with any of this, they're just coincidences." He sighed. "I guess being trapped in here isn't all bad. At least we're not in any immediate danger."

"Thank God it's not in the elevator," she whispered with a shudder.

"You'd just try to beat the dickens out of it to make it move."

She couldn't muster a smile for that statement. "I just got a bit panicky."

"It's too bad the air-conditioning's shot," Coop said. "But we do have windows that open." There was a soft squeaking sound, and she turned to see him opening the windows beside him, one by one. "Winston Lee was famous for his use of windows, or so I was told. He likes space and airiness. And I'm surprised that he didn't figure out a way to have windows in the elevators.''

Dylan moved away from him, hating the familiarity in his words, as if they had been friends for a very long time. As she opened the three windows near her, a slight breeze invaded the room. But it was hot and sultry, and the noises from outside intruded even more, bringing a hint of acrid smoke with them.

When she stopped by the third window and stared out at the night, there was no escaping the memories of the last time she'd been here with Coop. Quickly she spoke to fill the void, to distract herself and get through this. "How's your job going?"

"It's on hold."

She glanced to her right through the shadows and saw Coop near the middle windows. He had turned toward her, one hand resting on the frame of the open window. The pale light from the partial moon that was rising barely touched his face, but she knew he was looking right at her. "What does that mean?"

"I messed up a bit back, and I'm waiting to find out if I can still do the job or not."

She touched her tongue to her lips, remembering the way he walked in at first, the limp, the tentative way he used his right leg. "What happened?"

"An accident, a failure in the brake system of the prototype I was testing."

"How bad was the accident?" she asked in a tight voice.

"You know the old saying," he replied as he turned from her and moved to the chair by her purse. As he sank down in it, he said on an exhale, "Any accident you walk away from isn't all bad." He settled back in the chair, holding his right leg straight, and he actually chuckled—a sound that ran painfully over her nerves. "You of all people should know that."

How could he laugh about it when just the idea of him being in an accident made her chest clench? He could have died and she never would have known. That thought stunned her with its intensity. A world without Coop in it. And she'd had no idea at all that it could have been a reality. She unconsciously touched her stomach, the baby inside her becoming more precious to her all the time. "But you'll be all right, won't you?"

"As good as I can get. Brokaw's been joking around about me setting off metal detectors in airports with the pins in my leg."

"What if you can't work again?"

"Good question." He shrugged, a sharp movement in the darkness. "I'm reevaluating things right now, trying to figure out where my life is going. I'm sure you've gone through some of that yourself lately."

"Isn't that what life's all about? Change, adjusting, reevaluating?"

"I always thought life was to be lived, not analyzed, but sometimes you're forced to stop and regroup. You don't have any options." He was silent for a long moment before he spoke again. "Can I ask you something?"

Her legs felt weak, and she held on to the frame of the window. "What?"

"Why are you doing this?"

"I told you, I was checking things out to make sure the workmen—"

"No, I mean, the child. Why are you having it?"

She held so tightly to the window frame that her hand was starting to ache. "Actually, I asked myself that...for a while. Then, somewhere along the way, I knew I was going to have it. I don't know when it happened, but it just did."

"No major epiphany?"

"No," she said, but in that instant she knew the true epiphany in her life was right now—a moment of clarity that came without warning; a moment as great as any ever could be. As she looked at him through the darkness and felt the baby shift, she knew that there was no other way this could have been. The baby was a part of Coop, and part of her love for the man.

She loved Coop.

It was so simple now, and yet it had taken Dylan months to recognize. It stunned her. In all the time she'd thought about Coop, she could admit that she was attracted to him, that he fascinated her, that he stirred her and excited her. But at this moment, she knew that she had loved him all the time. Maybe that was why she'd kept the baby and maybe that was why there was a grief inside her that she doubted would ever leave when she thought that he could have died and she would never have known.

"So, you're married and pregnant and going to be famous for your work." His voice sounded tight. "You've got everything."

She knew how wrong that statement was, but there was nothing she could do about it. She knew she had to settle for having *nearly* everything. "Do *you* have everything?"

He turned away from her to look out at the night. "Right now, what I really want is something to drink."

If she weren't pregnant, she knew she wouldn't mind a good stiff drink herself. "There's a restaurant on the third floor, but it's not even set up. Oh, there's an executive lounge area just off the outer office. I saw a refrigerator in there." She needed space, and she was going to take the opportunity. "I'll go and see if there's anything in it."

She turned and started to walk between the chair and the windows to get to the door. But someway, somehow, near the chair, she tripped. Nothing was there, but she felt her foot snag, then she was falling sideways. She threw out her arms, trying to catch herself, and just before she hit the floor, she heard her name called.

Coop had never felt more helpless in his life. He'd twisted in the chair when he heard Dylan gasp. Then, before he could do anything, he saw her pitch forward and into the shadows.

He scrambled out of the chair, paying for the fast movement with pain shooting up his leg and into his hip. He gasped at the shards of agony, sucking in air, but he didn't stop. "Dylan!" he shouted as he grabbed at the back of his chair and pushed against it to propel himself in the right direction.

Even in the shadows he could see her on the floor, on her side, not moving, and for a horrifying moment, he knew a fear that far outweighed the fear he'd felt just before the crash. He cursed the accident and all the damage it had done to his bad leg. He'd barely managed to get to Dylan before his leg gave out and he half fell, half sat on the floor beside her.

"Dylan, Dylan!" he gasped as he braced himself with one hand by her shoulders to hold his weight, and with the other hand he touched her cheek.

It was silky and reassuringly warm, but she didn't move. He cupped her chin, gently easing her face around so he could see her, and he felt her shudder as she exhaled. "Oh, no," she breathed, then exhaled again. "No."

He leaned down, close to her, trying to see her and cursing the darkness. "Please, look at me. Open your eyes."

He felt her chin tremble slightly, then her eyes slowly opened. "Coop?"

"Just be real still. Don't move. I'll get someone. Or find someone." He didn't have a clue what he was going to do, but he knew he had to do something—fast. "Just be still."

But she didn't do what he said. Her hands moved up to her stomach, and she pressed the palms down with her fingers splayed on her swollen belly. She took a deep breath through her nose, then exhaled with a shudder. "Oh, Coop, the baby, it's not moving." He could hear the unsteadiness in her voice. "I...I'm scared."

So was he. "Just lie very still. Don't move. I'll...I'll get the phone and try to call for help. You just stay right there."

"There can't be anything wrong. There can't be," she breathed. "I mean, I just tripped. Tori was in a real accident and she was two weeks late and A.J. was healthy as a horse." She started making slow circles on her stomach. "Come on, in there, do something. Let me know you're okay."

"Are you in pain?"

"It's not me." She gave a shuddering breath. "Come on. A kick, anything. I don't care." Right then, her hand jerked on her stomach, and she was suddenly laughing softly. "Oh, thank God. Yes, that's it. Thank you, thank you," she whispered as she patted her stomach gently.

"It...it moved?" Coop asked.

"The baby's okay, I think." She exhaled in a rush. "I've never been so scared."

"It's not going to do anything crazy like come early, is it?"

"I hope not. I don't think so. When Tori went into labor, she was in terrible pain for almost twenty-four hours before she had A.J. They even sent her home once because they thought she was in false labor, but she went back six hours later."

He didn't want a blow-by-blow of her sister's birthing saga. All he wanted to know was that Dylan wasn't hurt. "Can you move?"

She actually chuckled unsteadily at that. "I think so, but if you've got cartwheels in mind, you're way out of luck."

He wasn't in any mood for joking, and he eased back. He grabbed the arm of the chair and tugged it sharply toward him. The motion knocked the phone off the purse, scooting it onto the carpet toward the windows and close enough so he could reach it. Then he sank back, moving enough to use the other chair as a backrest, and eased his bad leg straight in front of him to try and alleviate some of the pain.

He flipped the phone on. "I'll try to get someone up here," he said and quickly called 911. But all he got was a recording that all lines were busy, and to hold for the next operator. "Damn it all," he snarled.

"The only help I need right now is help from you to sit up. Then I'll be fine."

He was way out of his depth and he knew it. Another man's wife, another man's child, and he was responsible for both of them until the power came back on. He didn't like the feeling of that at all, yet perversely there was a part of him that felt what could have been jealousy over this phantom husband and father. The man had Dylan. And Coop knew what that was like—or at least he had for a few fleeting moments.

"What's your home number?" he asked. "I'll call your husband and see what he wants to do."

"No, please, don't," she said as she slowly turned onto her side and pressed one hand to the carpeting. "He . . . he'll just worry."

Welcome to the crowd, Coop thought, but said, "Are you sure?"

"Absolutely," she replied. "Right now, all I want is to sit up."

When she started to get up, he moved to help her, grabbing her hand in his and giving her leverage to get to a sitting position. Her hand felt slender and delicate in his as her fingers curled around his hand. Then she was up and had moved back against the bottom part of the windows with the night behind her.

When she let go of his hand and settled against the glass, he fought the overwhelming urge to pull her to him. He'd never felt terribly protective of anything or anyone in his life, not even of himself, but right now he wanted to protect Dylan from all the bad in the world, from all the pain and the ugliness out there.

If he could have stood at that moment, he would have offered to go looking for those drinks, but he knew better than to try to use his leg yet. He pushed himself back until he was leaning against the chair behind him, and he eased his bad leg out in front of him.

He clenched his teeth as he pressed a hand to his thigh and the pain there. "This blackout has to be over soon."

"I hope so," she said softly.

He couldn't help looking up at her. With the night behind her, she seemed so vulnerable, so insubstantial. The shadows hid everything but the delicate lines of her throat and the gentle rise and fall of her shoulders with each breath she took. Then she shifted and he could see her slip a hand behind her spine and lean back against it. "You said you weren't in pain."

"It's just a bit of a backache."

"From the fall?"

"No, I've had this most of the day. Probably just from being pregnant." She exhaled softly. "Actually, the baby's being pretty calm."

"And that's good?"

"It's better than the dropkicks that come at the most inopportune times. You remember Mr. Dytmyer who chaired the committee for this project? The one who called to tell me I'd won the bid?"

He remembered very well. "Sure."

"Well, I was talking to the committee a month or so ago, and right in the middle of my speech the baby kicked me right under the ribs and the chicken they served for lunch didn't stay down. Trust me, I'm very thankful when the baby's being good and quiet."

He found it easier to talk like this, in the dark, with distance between them. "Do you know what it is?"

"No, I didn't ask. But I wish I had."

"Do you have any names in mind? Maybe something after literary greats. Byron Shelley? Emily Dickinson? Dr. Seuss?"

"Dr. Seuss?"

How easy it was to tease her, make a joke. God, it felt good—for a while, but he knew it wouldn't last, any more than the blackout would. "A great American poet. Surely you've read *The Cat in the Hat* or *Green Eggs and Ham?*"

"Have you?"

"Way back in my misbegotten youth. I always sort of liked the Grinch."

"Not my favorite, and I think I'll pass on Seuss and stick to more traditional names."

"So, what names are you thinking about?"

She rested her hands on her stomach in an action so gentle and protective, Coop had only one thought: How he wished her touch was on him.

Chapter Twelve

"I really haven't thought that much about names," Dylan said.

"What about your husband? Doesn't he have any favorites?"

"No." A siren cut through the night, its piercing wail very close below.

Coop glanced past Dylan out the window and despite his low vantage point, he could see the darkness in the distance dotted with emergency lights. "Where do you live now?"

"In the same house, but the front room's my workspace until I can afford a separate office."

"I thought you'd get an office in this building."

"I couldn't afford it."

"You didn't marry a rich man?"

"That wasn't a criterion," she said, and he could hear the tightness in her voice.

"What were the criteria?"

She said almost offhandedly, "The usual."

He wasn't going to ask what "the usual" meant to her. He didn't really want to know, even though he'd asked.

"He must be worried sick about you."

"He knows I can take care of myself," she said. "And I'm doing okay."

"If you can manage to avoid any more accidents," he said, surprised that he could actually joke right then.

She laughed softly. "Remember, I told you when we first met that I tend to have accidents."

"Yes, you did." He remembered. He remembered too well. And he didn't want to. He shifted, easing onto one side to reach back and grab the chair arm. It was time to get some distance, even at the price of more pain in his bad leg. "I'm still thirsty, but this time I'll go to see if there's anything to drink."

He managed to get to his feet, enduring the discomfort until he could grip the back of the chair and glance down at Dylan. "So, where do I go?"

"Is your leg sore?"

"It works." He forced himself to let go of the chair and stand as straight as he could. "Now, where do I go?"

"There's a sort of executive lounge just off the outer room to the right."

"Okay, just relax, and I'll be right back," he said as he turned and let go of the chair to head for the door. His leg hurt like hell, but he managed to make it into the outer office.

Side windows in the reception room let in enough light from the moon that he could make out a door partway along the wall on the right. He didn't bother trying to minimize his limp as he made his way to the door then he opened it and was faced with total darkness. He automatically reached for the light switch by the door, and flipped it up before he caught himself. There were no windows and the air was oppressively hot.

"I can't see a thing," he called back to Dylan. "Give me an idea where I'm going."

"There're cupboards and two sinks like a vanity to the left, then all the way to the back, there's another sink, some more counters, cupboards and a small refrigerator." Her voice came to him in the darkness, and he felt his stomach clench. Damn it, he almost wished he hadn't seen her car downstairs and hadn't come up here and hadn't seen her again, or felt so much pleasure at the sight of her—only to have it turn to ashes when he saw her pregnancy and found out she was married.

He put out a hand to his left, felt the face of closed cupboards, then a counter, smooth and warm, a sink, a thick stack of towels, another sink, and finally the back of the room. By the time he felt a metal door and knew he'd found the refrigerator, his shirt was soaked and sticking to his skin.

He opened the door and a wave of welcome coolness spilled out, then he felt inside. He almost knocked over a plastic bottle, grabbed at it and took it out. The only other thing in the fridge was a box. He took that, too, and turned, heading back to the suggestion of light in the outer office.

After being in such total darkness, he could see better out here and when he looked toward the open office door, he stopped. He could see into the room. He could see Dylan against the windows, and in that moment, he tasted real bitterness on his tongue. She was married, having a child, and he was too late.

If timing was everything, he thought as he stepped forward, then he was left with next to nothing. He moved carefully on his bad leg, heading for the windows where Dylan was sitting framed against the backdrop of the night. As she looked up at him, her features softly blurred by the darkness, for the first time that he could remember, he felt as if he'd lost something—something he had never really had.

"We got lucky," he said, watching the way she looked up. "The refrigerator was still cool inside, and there was—" He held up the bottle toward the windows and could vaguely make out clear liquid. "It looks like water."

He held the bottle out to her. "Test it first. Don't take my word for it." When she took the bottle from him, he drew back quickly, not wanting to make any direct contact. He wasn't sure he could stand feeling her touch on him without being able to have more.

He held the box up to try to see what it was. In the dimness, he could almost make out a logo. "More luck. Cupcakes, cream filled. A veritable feast. What more could you ask for?''

''Air-conditioning,'' Dylan said as she opened the bottle.

''Sorry, there isn't any of that around here.'' He put the box of cupcakes on the arm of the chair behind him, then undid his shirt buttons. He tugged the shirt free of his waistband and pulled the damp material away from his skin. Then he eased back down into the chair facing Dylan and reached for the box. He opened it and took out two cupcakes in foil wrapping. ''How about a snack?''

She tipped her head back, taking a tentative drink, then drank more before she lowered the bottle. ''It's water and it's cool,'' she said. ''I'm not hungry, just thirsty.'' She held the bottle out to him. ''Do you want a drink?''

He looked down at the foil-wrapped cakes in his hand, then put them back in the package and tossed the box onto the floor by the chair. He almost refused a drink, even though he was thirsty, because the idea of drinking after her seemed disturbingly intimate to him.

But he accepted the bottle without touching her, then took a long drink of the cool water before he sank back in the chair. He rested the bottle on his thigh, and looked at her through the shadows.

''How are you feeling?''

"Hot. A bit claustrophobic." She hesitated, then abruptly asked him, "How did you know I was up here?"

"I saw a car and thought it was yours... at first."

"Why were you driving around here?"

"I wasn't." He could stick to the truth on this. "Brokaw was driving and going to a restaurant nearby. At least, he was dragging me along with him." He put the bottle on the floor by the cupcake box, then sat back, pressing one hand to his right thigh. "I didn't know he'd turned onto this street until I looked up and saw the buildings. Then I saw the car. I figured out it wasn't your BMW but I was here—so I came to see what you did with the building."

"So, you were just in the neighborhood and dropped in... to say hi?"

He knew how ridiculous that sounded, yet the truth was even more ridiculous now that he was here. How could he tell her that he'd come to see her—to see if they could start all over again? Not when she was married and pregnant.

"Something like that," he hedged.

"Well, you got yourself in a mess by stopping, didn't you?" she said softly. "If you hadn't come in, you'd be at a party right now and probably having a good time with cold drinks and good food, even if the lights are all out."

He stared at her as he realized he really didn't want to be anywhere else—not at a party, or in Spain, or anywhere else in the world. He'd come back to see

Dylan, then walked away but hadn't made it. Fate had stopped him dead in his tracks—again.

"Just what I need is to sit in the dark with drunks," he muttered.

"So, you're sitting in the dark with a pregnant woman who can't avoid accidents," she countered.

"As long as you sit right there, there won't be any more accidents."

"Good idea," she murmured as she stretched her legs out on the carpet and rested her head back against the window. "How did you know I was up here?" she asked, the question coming from nowhere.

"I didn't. I thought you might be up here, but..." He shrugged. "I thought I'd look."

"And if I hadn't been here?"

He knew he should say he would have left and gone to the party, but that wasn't the truth at all. He would have kept looking, probably gotten a taxi and gone to her house to wait for her to return. "I could have admired what you've done."

There was silence in the room for a long moment, then he heard Dylan sigh. "It's so hot."

"California, where it never rains and never gets too hot."

She laughed softly at his words. "Tourist propaganda. The truth is, it rains, and it's hot."

"And it has earthquakes."

"Oh, please, don't even mention that. With the way things are going, we might start to shake anytime now."

Coop fingered his thigh and studied her shadowy face. He could almost make out the line of her jaw, the way her cheekbones were defined, her full bottom lip. He was disgusted by the way his body began to tighten. God, she was married and pregnant and she still stirred him on a physical level. It was absurd, but a reality.

"Yeah, that's all we need," he muttered and glanced past her out at the night sky. The sounds outside that filtered into the room did nothing to ease a growing tension in the hot air.

"The water?"

He looked back at her and she had her hand held out toward him. For a crazy moment, he thought she wanted him to take her hand, to pull her to him, and the need in him to hold her was so sharply defined that it almost made his chest hurt. Then he realized she was asking for a drink. He held the bottle out to her and tried to shake off his insanity as she took a deep drink. When she would have given it back to him, he waved it off. "Keep it. You need it more than I do."

She touched the bottle to her cheek and slowly rolled it on her skin to try to capture some of its coolness. "So, did Brokaw ever get his car fixed properly?"

"That Mercedes was put down for the count and he's driving a Porsche now."

"What?"

"He traded it in on a Porsche. It was easier than having it repaired. I think once the Mercedes was wounded, he lost interest in it, so he got rid of it."

"After all that money for the repairs, and he was looking for a sports car all the time?" she asked, her tone obviously disbelieving.

"That's the way Brokaw is—always looking for another car. He's into image. He loves cars, and he decided that he wanted a Porsche, so he got one."

She exhaled, and he could see her bangs ruffle from her own breath. He'd said he liked her short hair, but if truth be told, he missed the long mane that she'd had before. "It must be nice," she said.

"How's your BMW?"

"Gone. I just bought a new car."

"Your husband buy it for you?"

She took her time drinking more water, then rested the bottle on her lap. "No, I wouldn't ask him to pay for it."

"You'd think he would anyhow. The same way you'd think he'd be down here to find out if you're okay."

"How do you know he isn't? The elevators aren't working and the stairs are closed off. What do you think he should do, fly up to the windows and peek in?"

He didn't understand the touch of sarcasm in her voice, not any more than he understood the anger he was starting to feel for a man he'd never met. If Dylan was his, he would have moved heaven and earth to get to her, to make sure she was all right. "He could have called on your cellular phone."

"He probably can't get through."

"Sure," he muttered. "He's a knight in shining armor, riding to your rescue—if the elevators worked."

"He's not Superman," she said sharply.

"Obviously."

She put the bottle of water on the carpet with a sharp thud, then moved to one side and got to her knees. Before he could get up, she was on her feet and turning her back on him to face the windows.

With the light from the fires and the growing moon behind her, he caught a glimpse of her legs silhouetted through the fine material of her dress. The way he had when he first saw her in this room.

He watched her, letting that image filter into his soul, but he didn't move. If he did, he knew he would go to her, touch her, hold her, and it killed him that those feelings just grew instead of filtering away.

"My husband is none of your business," she whispered without turning back to him.

"You're right. I don't have any business asking you anything about him or criticizing him."

She stayed silent, and he thought she was going to just ignore the whole thing. Then he realized that her shoulders were trembling. He struggled to his feet and went over to her, but didn't touch her. "Hey, what's going on?"

She shrugged, in a fluttery, vulnerable motion. "Nothing. Everything. I don't know. Hormones."

"Listen, I didn't mean to upset you. You're right, I had no business saying anything about anything."

"This is all so... so crazy," she whispered.

"It could be worse."

"Worse than this heat and no power and... and... being trapped up here?"

He heard her take a small, shuddering breath and impulsively reached out to touch her shoulder. He gently eased her back and turned her to face him. In the darkness, he looked down at her and emotions that defied description rushed through him—protectiveness, need, desire, and something that he couldn't name; a sense of something that bordered on homecoming.

Tentatively he framed her face with his hands, smoothing her flushed skin with the balls of his thumbs. "Everything's going to be just fine. I promise. The lights will be back on soon, and we'll have air-conditioning and your husband is probably downstairs right now, ready to take you to your birthday party."

"Oh, Coop," she breathed with a shudder.

"Hey, come on, he'll fly up here if he has to," he said, knowing he would give it a damn good try if he was her husband and knew she was trapped up here.

She shook her head slowly and with such a touch of vulnerability that something in him snapped. An anger at a man he'd never seen, a man whose name he didn't even know, burned in him. Something was wrong, very wrong, and Dylan was in pain. He could hate the man. "Dylan, love, it's not that bad."

Even in the dark he could see the tears and feel them on his hands, and he knew he would do anything to stop them. He brushed at the moisture, smoothing it away from her skin, then said, "Can I have this dance?"

Her tongue touched the tears on her lips, then she whispered, "Wh-what?"

"Dance." He took her hand, laced his fingers with hers, then slipped his other hand around behind her. And it was as if time had slipped backward. A dark office, holding Dylan, and without planning, he started to hum softly a song that had stayed with him for eight months—"You Send Me."

He felt Dylan tremble slightly, and he drew her closer. The simple swaying from side to side hurt his knee like crazy, but he realized he would go through any amount of pain to hold her like this. It was what he'd wanted to do since he'd found her at the windows in the shadows. She gave a shuddering sigh, and he realized he wasn't prepared for the way she came to him. Her arms circled his waist and she buried her face in his chest where his shirt parted.

All movement stopped as he absorbed the feel of her against him, and he had to close his eyes tightly when his whole being began to respond to what he had in his arms. "Oh, Dylan..." He bit his lip hard as her hands spread on his back. Nothing had changed. Nothing. He wanted her so badly that his body ached for her.

"Coop?" she breathed in a voice that was almost inaudible to him. "Why did you come back?"

With her in his arms, there was no way he could hedge this time. "To see you." He pressed a kiss to the silkiness of her hair, then the full truth was there. "I came back to see if there was any way we could start over again."

She was very still. Then she eased back and he knew she was looking at him. "What?"

When he opened his eyes, he knew he shouldn't have. Her head was tipped back, her eyes were on him, and he found it all but impossible to breathe in the hot air of the room.

"God, I missed you so much," he admitted with raw truth and knew right then that he wasn't just in lust with this woman. It wasn't just a physical desire for her that drew him back to her. It was something that was as real as it was perverse. He'd walked away from her, and now it was too late. But he loved her. And a pain he'd never felt before settled deep inside him, and he silently cursed whatever force had let him walk away from her eight months ago.

Dylan knew that the heat and her need and probably her hormones were playing havoc with her sanity. Being in the room with Coop was bad enough, but to have him talking about some husband who wasn't close to being real, was hard to take. Then he'd touched her and held her. The soft humming vibrated through her, bonding the present with the past, and she let herself go to him.

She leaned against him, inhaling his scent, letting his heat overlap the heat of the room, and she never wanted to leave his arms. Then he'd spoken in a low, rough voice, but the words he said couldn't be true.

"I came back to see if there was any way we could start all over again." She slowly moved back and tried to look into his face. She swallowed, then touched her tongue to the saltiness of tears on her lips before she could manage to say, "What do you mean, start over again?" She desperately needed to know.

"You remember. Hello, I'm Cooper Reeves and I'm in San Diego because I couldn't stop thinking about you." His thumbs stilled on her cheeks. "I couldn't."

She closed her eyes for a long moment as she absorbed what could have been, what might have been. His hands let her go as she heard him utter a low, vibrating oath. When she opened her eyes, he'd turned from her, standing still in the shadows, no more than a few feet from her.

"I really blew it," he breathed hoarsely. "I don't know what I expected, but I didn't expect all of this. Married. Dammit. My timing stinks, doesn't it?"

It was like a dream to her—to hear his words, to know he'd come back after all to find her. And a nightmare. "What if I wasn't married? What then?"

"Stop it!" he retorted. "I'm hot and my leg hurts like hell, and I'm not in any mood to deal in fairy tales." He turned and she could see his face twisted in a frown and his skin sheened with moisture. "You got married, Dylan. Playing what-if games won't change that, no matter what problems you're having with your husband.''

She hated the lies, and knew that the only way to put all this to rest was to stop them. She clenched her hands tightly at her sides. "I'm not married. I never have been."

"What in the—"

"I'm not married."

She was shocked when he abruptly reached out and took her by her shoulders. His skin was hot against hers, and his fingers pressed into her shoulders, causing something hovering just this side of real pain. "What in the hell are you talking about?"

"I thought—" She shook her head. "I thought it was best if people thought I was married. I never meant to—" No words would come that made sense of any of this except "I'm sorry."

"There's no husband?"

She couldn't say a thing, so she simply shook her head.

"Damn you," he swore, his hands tightening on her.

For a horrible moment, she thought he was going to push her away and leave. "I'm sorry."

With a low groan, he pulled her to him, and when his mouth captured hers, the rest of the world with all its problems and pain might never have existed. As soon as she felt his lips on hers, as soon as his taste was on her tongue, nothing made any difference except being right here, right now, holding on to him. When his arms circled her, she felt as if she was being welcomed into a safe place, a place she'd been looking for ever since he left, months ago.

For that moment she let herself go and held to him, opening her mouth in invitation. And the next thing she knew, she was lost. The kiss was deep and intense, a ravishing of her that she welcomed with her whole being. Passion didn't need time to grow. It came white-hot and immediate. It burned through her, stunning her, yet thrilling her.

She fumbled awkwardly to push aside his shirt, needing the feel of skin on skin, and as the damp material fell away, she spread her hands on his chest. Her palms pressed against the silky heat of his skin, the obvious tension of his muscles, and she wished she could be absorbed into him, that he could inhale and she would be part of him.

But before any sort of fantasy could become reality, another reality brought everything to a halt. The baby kicked, and kicked hard. It was literally between the two of them, and couldn't be denied. Everything stopped. She'd forgotten about the child—something that seemed like an impossibility—but all she'd been thinking of was Coop, of touching and holding him.

But now he was drawing back, and she pulled her hands away from his chest. Her palms were damp from the moisture on his skin, and her hands shook as she pulled them back to her stomach. She stared at Coop as the connection between the two of them was broken, and she could tell he was staring at her. At her stomach.

"The baby." His voice was so low she barely heard him.

"A dropkick," she said, wishing the words had come out in an even tone instead of in a tremulous whisper. "I guess being married wasn't the biggest hurdle, was it?"

She asked the question and she knew she wanted him to say, "A baby, how terrific!" and tell her that her being pregnant wasn't a problem. Then she could tell him he was the father and he'd be ecstatic instead of repulsed and angry.

But that was real fantasy. The reality was him staring at her stomach as if he couldn't believe what he saw.

"What about the father?" he finally asked.

An insidious spark of hope that she'd allowed to spring to life for a brief moment was gone, and she felt vaguely sick. Her back ached, and she wished she could just go to sleep and wake up to find out there were lights, and coolness, and that Coop had never come back.

"I don't want to talk about this," she murmured.

"Is he in the picture at all?" he persisted.

She hugged her arms around herself and exhaled with real weariness. "Why?"

"I want to know."

"Do you want to take over and play at being a father?" she asked, and she couldn't stop the sarcasm that crept into her voice.

The silence in the room was as deafening as the sirens had been earlier until he said, "I wouldn't begin to know how. Besides, it's his kid."

"So? What difference does it make? He doesn't want anything to do with the baby."

"Oh, man." She could see him run a hand around the back of his neck. "He just took off?"

She was holding on to her arms so tightly that her fingers felt numb. But words came that she regretted almost as much as she knew she had to say them. "What would you have done if some woman said, 'Oh, by the way, I'm pregnant. I'm having a little alien who's going to spit up on you and cry a lot and probably drive you crazy?'"

"That doesn't have anything to do with any of this," he muttered.

Dylan felt absolutely claustrophobic; her chest was so tight, she could scarcely breathe. She turned and grabbed the edge of the open window as she leaned toward it to take breaths of the hot, outside air. She needed to get out of here, but there was no escape. The city was still dark, lost in the throes of the emergency below, and she was lost in this emergency. "Forget it," she said.

"How can I, after what just happened?"

She tried to take in air to ease the tightness in her and she wished she could banish his taste from her tongue. "That doesn't change a thing," she managed to say.

"You wanted that as much as I did." His words were edged with hoarseness.

She couldn't deny that, so she ignored it. "I don't want to talk about any of this. I'm hot and miserable, and I just want to forget it happened."

"I wish I could," she heard him rasp behind her.

"Well, work on it. Babies don't just go away. They're real human beings, and just wishing won't make things any different." She closed her eyes to fight the tears of frustration as she admitted to herself that even if she could wish this all away, she wouldn't. She loved Coop. She would live with that for the rest of her life, but she loved this child, too.

"Can't you work out something with the father?"

She couldn't take this any longer. Without a word, she turned and tried to see where her cellular phone was. Then she saw the flashing Standby light and bent down to retrieve it. She flipped it open and hit the numbers for the guard station downstairs. But before she knew what was happening, Coop had jerked the phone away from her and tossed it onto the chair.

When she would have turned to reach for it, Coop had her by the hand, stopping her. She cautiously turned to look at him. His hand all but covered hers, his fingers gentle, but restrictive, and she felt slightly light-headed.

"What are you doing?" she demanded, anger the only barrier she could think of to use against his closeness and her own needs.

"Trying to talk to you. Trying to make some sense out of this insanity." She jerked free of his hold on her, and forced herself not to rub her hand and try to rid herself of the lingering sensation of his touch.

She pushed her hands behind her back. "Maybe there isn't any sanity in this whole mess."

He came even closer, and if she tried to go to the windows, she would have brushed against him. She didn't want to take that chance, so she stayed where she was.

"I came back here with some vague idea about needing to see you again. I just knew that I had to come. Then I get here and I can see you're pregnant and think you're married, and I was ready to leave. I knew it was a dead end. Then this blackout stopped that, and I finally find out that you're not married."

"But I'm pregnant," she said, her jaw clenched and tight. "Very pregnant."

"I know, I know. God, how can I forget that? But I'm trying to figure out what to do."

"There's nothing to do. You've been very clear about how you feel about kids." She took a shuddering breath. "You told me you broke up a marriage because you didn't want any kids."

He raked his fingers through his hair and exhaled in a rush. "Oh, God, that was just one of several reasons, and maybe just an excuse. I don't know. It seems as if that was all from another life."

"You didn't want kids, did you?"

"Hell, no. I was gone all the time. I was pushing life to the edge and loving it. All I needed was a child depending on me. I probably shouldn't have been married then, either."

"Being a father wasn't an option, was it?"

"No. I can't deny that."

"And you haven't changed, have you?"

"I haven't even thought about it," he said with a rough sigh as he turned from her. She never took her eyes off him as he glanced out the windows, and she could see his profile, the tension in his jaw and the way his hair was sticking damply to his neck and temples. "God, I just found out about all of this. I'm trying to figure it out."

She braced herself, then said what she had to say. "You don't have to. Don't even try. When the power comes back on, leave."

He took a deep, rough breath. "No."

"Why not?" she demanded, desperately needing to know.

When he slowly turned to her, silently he put out his hand and brushed her cheek with the tips of his fingers. "Do you have to ask that?"

She bit her lip hard, the sensation of his touch on her cheek compelling and riveting. "Yes," she whispered.

"I can't." He gently smoothed her hair back from her cheek, then lightly ran the tip of his finger over the curve of her ear. "I thought I could. I thought I could walk out and keep going if you didn't want to start again."

"You left," she breathed. "The only reason you're here is because you got trapped by the blackout. You saw I was pregnant and took off."

His hand moved to the nape of her neck, gently cupping it with his palm. "Oh, I tried to. God knows, I tried. But you know what? I think I was almost thankful to be stopped."

She could barely stand his touch on her. "Coop, don't do this."

His hand trembled, but he didn't let her go. "I have to. It's a mess, a horrible mess, but there has to be a way out of it. Some rational way to work around the problems."

Problems? The only problem was literally right between them. The baby. "How?"

"We could talk to the father together and see if he'll be reasonable. Maybe he'll want to be part of the kid's life, maybe even want to share custody."

"Stop," she cried and jerked back from his seductive touch. "Just stop. He doesn't want the baby. He hates kids. He never wanted kids. He thinks they're like aliens." She stopped her words on a gulp and stared wide-eyed at Coop. She hadn't meant to say that. Never.

But the words hung between them, and she knew that the damage was done when Coop uttered, "Oh, no."

Chapter Thirteen

Coop felt as if he had been hit in the middle by a Mack truck. He exhaled on a rush, and couldn't move. Even when Dylan moved back, partially receding into the shadows, he couldn't go after her.

"No," he managed to say. "We used protection."

She laughed unsteadily, but there was no humor in it. "Ninety-five-percent effective. They never tell you that means that you've got a five-percent chance of it not working."

"Oh, man," he uttered.

"Believe me, I was shocked, too. Just don't worry about any of this. We don't want anything from you. We'll be okay."

His middle churned, and his hands clenched so tightly he could feel his nails digging into his palms. "Why in the hell didn't you tell me?"

"How could I have told you? I didn't even have a phone number for you. Jeb Brokaw isn't in the book, and you didn't come back in January. Besides, you hate kids." He could hear the edge of bitterness in her voice. "Why would I have told you? There was no reason to tell you anything."

"So you lied to me?"

"I did what I had to do."

His leg ached horribly, and he eased back, then dropped down in the chair. He stretched his bad leg out in front of him and ran a hand roughly over his face. "So you lied about being married and you lied about the child. What else should I know?"

"That this isn't anything to do with you anymore."

"If I'd only known," he muttered.

She was behind him now and her voice came out of the darkness. "If you'd known, would you have told me to get rid of it, take it out of the picture? Sorry, that wasn't even an option for me."

"You don't know what I would have done," he countered.

"I had a good idea."

That was more than he had. He let his head sink back against the soft cushions on the back of the chair, and he stared out the window at the night. A child. It took his breath away on so many levels. Dylan's child. A child he never wanted, never even considered wanting.

Oddly, it was a relief it wasn't another man's child, but that didn't mean all this was any easier on him now. He stared out at the stars and the cloudless night sky. He couldn't begin to fathom it.

But Dylan spoke up quickly from behind him. "*My* child," she said tightly. "It's just me and the baby."

Her words effectively shut him out, making him feel isolated and very much alone. And he hated it. He heard her move and he glanced to his right, seeing her step through the shadows and back to the windows. She gripped the window's edge and looked down at the street below.

"You didn't do it alone," he said.

He saw her start slightly at his words, then one of her hands went behind her to press at the small of her back. "Why don't we pretend I did," she said, without looking at him. "It's sure going to make things easier for all of us."

He couldn't take his eyes off her—the way the strange light from the moon and the city defined the line of her bare shoulders, the way she lifted her chin just a bit, the way her stomach was swollen with his child. And in that moment, he knew he needed her. Not just physically, not even just emotionally. He needed her in his life. It was so simple.

He narrowed his eyes and tried to absorb the simplicity of his realization. He could look at her and admit that he loved her. And he didn't want to walk away. He wouldn't. She sighed and rubbed at her back, making her stomach even more noticeable, and it all fell into place. Him, Dylan and the child. His child. A child he'd never thought he would ever want—or need.

God, he had the feeling that the world had been tipped on its ear, then put back in place, only to be tilted again. Nothing had been the same since he'd met Dylan. Nothing. And he knew that he didn't want to go back to before that time.

"Dylan?"

She didn't look at him as she whispered, "Please, just let go."

He grabbed the arms of the chair and levered himself to his feet. Ignoring the pain in his leg, he crossed to where she stood, touched her shoulders, and rested his hands on her damp skin. He could sense that her first instinct was to hit his hand away, but she didn't. She didn't look at him, either.

"You've changed a lot since we met," he said.

He could feel her take an unsteady breath. "I think that's pretty obvious."

"Well, you're not alone," he whispered, controlling the urge to pull her back against him and hold on for dear life.

"Coop, I can't—"

"No, you can't," he said. "And I can't. Not alone. Why should we each be alone, when we could be together?"

He felt her take a sharp breath, then slowly turn. He never let go completely. Even when she was facing him, he kept his hands on her shoulders. "What?"

"You're different, not just because of your short hair or being pregnant, but you're different."

"Don't analyze me. Not now."

"I'm not. I'm just trying to figure out how all this happened, how things changed completely."

"I think we went through this before. It's called 'life.'"

"Damn straight, and it's our life."

"No..."

"Oh, yes."

She raised her hands and covered her face as if she couldn't stand to look at him, but didn't have the energy to pull away from him. He shifted and gently touched her hands to ease them down so he could gaze at her. "Oh, God, you're beautiful. Just beautiful."

She looked up at him and he could see her chin trembling. "I can't take this, Coop, I can't."

"Just listen to one last thing, then I'll walk out of here when the power's back on and I won't bother you again. You can live the life you want to live." He'd never begged for anything in his life, never, but right then he knew he would beg if he had to. "Please?"

She closed her eyes tightly, then opened them, their expression lost in the darkness.

He took a very unsteady breath and said words that he'd never thought he would say to anyone. "I love you. I probably have from the very first, and despite all of my words and denials, I think I could love this child."

She stood very still, not saying anything, and he had the horrible sensation that it was too little, too late. "Did you hear me?"

"Yes. I heard," she said flatly.

"I love you." Then he did something that shocked him, yet seemed very natural. He reached out and touched her stomach. He felt her flinch, but he didn't draw back. He pressed his palm lightly to her stomach and never took his eyes off her face. For a long moment, all he felt was her breathing. Then, from nowhere, he felt the child move—a small knob pushed against his hand. Then it was gone.

"Oh, God," he whispered, and an astonishing thing happened. He suddenly knew what it was to be connected, to be part of a whole. It was a place he'd never been before in his entire life, and he didn't want to ever leave it again.

"I have to know if you mean it," she said, and he knew she was crying. "I have to know."

He didn't hesitate as he pulled her into his arms. He rested his chin on her head and closed his eyes tightly. "Oh, yes, I mean it," he breathed.

She circled his waist with her arms, pressed her face into his chest and cried, the sobs shaking her body. He awkwardly brushed her hair and patted her back. "Hush, it's okay. It's okay," he whispered over and over again.

She sniffed, then rubbed her forehead against his chest and her voice was muffled against his skin. "You mean it," she murmured over and over again.

"You bet I do," he said without hesitation, and he tipped her face to look into her eyes.

The heat of the night was nothing compared to the heat this woman produced in him. And when he tasted her lips, and the saltiness of tears was there, he loved her with all his heart. "God, I want you," he breathed. "It seems like forever."

She pressed a kiss to his chest and whispered, "Oh, yes."

"Can you?" he asked, a tremor making his voice very unsteady when she spread her hands on his chest. "I mean, I don't want to hurt you... or the baby."

She kissed his nipple, sending shock waves through his body, then drew back and smiled up at him. And even the darkness couldn't hide the beauty in her expression. "Oh, it's okay."

"Are you sure?"

Dylan had never been more sure of anything in her life. Everything had fit together, neatly and perfectly, and even though she had come up here alone, she had found everything she needed. She lifted a hand to touch Coop's face, her fingertips brushing the beginnings of a new beard, and she loved the feel of him. "Very sure."

Coop brushed at her cheeks, smoothing away the tears, then he cupped her face and kissed her again.

The contact was deep and searching. Then his hands moved lower, and he cupped her full breasts. His touch was fire to her, consuming her, and she strained toward him. Her breasts were sensitive, and even through the thin material of her dress and the light bra, she could feel her nipples tightening.

His hands found her zipper and lowered it, then he eased the straps off her shoulders and the gauzy material of her sundress slipped down. Her bra was undone, and her breasts freed. He cupped their weight, his thumb and forefinger finding her nipples, and she moaned from the pleasure his touch gave her.

She wanted more, much more, and she skimmed her hands down over his abdomen to the snap on his jeans. She pulled at the denim, felt the fastener give, and found the evidence of his desire for her—a desire that was echoed in her.

Carefully, he eased her down onto the soft carpeting, and in the shadows dappled with moonlight, she rolled toward him, into his arms. It was as if they had never been parted. His touch, the feeling of him against her, was so familiar that it made her ache deep inside. Her hands explored him, and the sensations matched her memories, but when his hands pushed at the material of her dress, she knew that her body wasn't in his memory. Not this body. Not a body large and swollen with the child.

She covered his hand with hers, holding the thin material up to cover her stomach, but as he pushed it lower, he raised himself on one elbow and when she opened her eyes, she saw him looking at her. His gaze skimmed over her, lingering on her full breasts, then the swelling of her stomach. He touched her, cupping her breast, and lowered his head to kiss her nipple. His lips trailed down to her stomach, and she felt the heat of his breath against her skin.

She feared that he would turn from her, but that never happened. He raised his head, his shadowed eyes meeting hers, and his whispered voice made her tremble. "You're more beautiful than ever."

She realized then that she'd been holding back, despite his assurance that things were different, that he wanted her and the child. But now she felt no barriers. She wrapped her arms around his neck and drew him down to her, welcoming his touch and his kiss. And she could feel her body responding with an abandonment that shocked her.

Their contact was almost frantic, as if each was in the throes of a hunger that had built for a lifetime. Their touches were urgent and filled with need. And when she touched him, when she felt his hard strength, she wished she was small and slender and could easily sit astride him to let him fill her.

He lightly kissed her, then drew back. "Just take it easy. Just let it happen. We've got all the time in the world."

She touched his lips with the tips of her fingers and started to tell him he was right, that they could take all the time they wanted. But instead of those words, she found herself gasping. Pain radiated from her back to her stomach and almost doubled her over. "Oh, no," she gasped when the pain grew stronger and stronger.

"What?" Coop asked, moving back.

She curled into a fetal position, biting her lip hard until the pain started to diminish; then it was gone and she nearly collapsed onto her back. She took a deep, cleansing breath and whispered, "This can't be happening."

"What can't be happen—" He cut himself off, then echoed her earlier words, "Oh, no."

"Oh, yes," she gasped as another pain started. "It's the baby."

"I knew it. We shouldn't have tried to be close. As much as I want you, I didn't want to ever hurt you or the baby."

"Oh, Coop," she breathed.

"It's too early, isn't it?"

"Yes," she gasped again, then concentrated on breathing and riding it out. She knew Coop was talking to her, but she couldn't say a thing until the pain eased.

"I'm sorry," he said, and she shook her head.

"It's...it's not that. It's just happening, but it's all wrong. They said the baby would get really quiet for hours before labor started. They said that there would be easy pain before labor really started and the pain would be in my stomach, that I'd know when it was going to happen."

When Coop touched her face with his hand, her skin felt flushed and damp, and he knew a fear that was a living, painful thing. But not a fear for himself. A fear for Dylan and the child. His child. All he wanted was to have them safe and sound at the end of all this, and he didn't know a thing about labor or childbirth.

"Just tell me what to do."

"The phone," she breathed. "Try to call again."

He twisted to his right, found the phone on the chair, and pushed the Power button. Nothing happened. He hit the button again, over and over again, but there were no lights and no beeps. "It's not working," he muttered.

"Let me . . . let me see it." She took it, fiddled with the buttons, then sank back and let it fall to the carpet. "The battery's dead," she whispered.

He took the phone from her hand, then tossed it to one side and concentrated on Dylan. In the shadows he could see the sheen of moisture on her skin; her eyes were tightly closed and her hands spanned her stomach. "What now?"

"I wish I'd taken—" Her words were cut off by a sharp intake of air, then she started to breathe quickly while her hands made circles on her stomach.

He watched helplessly, wishing he knew something about what was going on. When she finally released a long, deep breath, he could see her whole body relax. "You wish you'd taken what?" he asked quickly before another pain could come.

"Classes. Natural childbirth classes. Tori tried to get me to sign up for the classes and I didn't want to go. I just wanted to be knocked out and wake up with it over." She actually laughed softly. "I guess there aren't any options now."

"Are you sure this is for real?" he asked, bending over her.

She looked up at him, her eyes dark and wide. "I don't know. Maybe—" Right then her face twisted and she gasped sharply, then took a series of rapid breaths. And when she finally relaxed, she looked up at him. "It feels real."

"Everything I know about this I saw in the movies," he said.

She laughed at that, too. "Oh, great. What a team—" Her words stopped on another gasp as her hold on his arm grew painful. "Oh, my," she whispered.

"What? What?"

"I think my water just broke."

That was one thing he understood. "Okay, we'll need . . . things. Uh, in the other room, there're towels and water. I have to go—"

"Oh, Coop—" Her body arched as another pain came full force.

"Okay, okay," he soothed, holding her hand while the pain reached its full force, then began to recede. "We can do this, love. We can do this. I promise you, everything's going to be all right."

He wasn't a religious man, but even as he said those words, he prayed that they were true. The feelings of fear and protectiveness and love were so new to him that he almost didn't recognize them. But he knew he would do anything it took to make sure Dylan and his child were both here and safe when the lights came back on.

He'd just found them, and he wouldn't lose them now.

Chapter Fourteen

Coop had lost all track of time. It could have been an eternity since all this started, or just minutes. But he knew that his whole world centered on this woman and this child fighting to come into it.

"Whew, whew, whew," Dylan breathed as the latest pain subsided.

Coop let go of her hand just long enough to reach for one of the towels he'd found in the executive lounge and wiped at the dampness on her face. Quickly he pressed a kiss to her forehead before he sank back on the carpet and reached for her hand again. "I love you, Dylan Bradford," he whispered, and her hand tightened on his.

"Boy, is our timing off," she said in a voice that was noticeably weaker than it had been earlier.

Coop was afraid. His gut twisted every time the pains came, and he did everything he could think to do. But he knew it wasn't enough. He had spread the towels, gotten her as comfortable as he could between pains, then he waited. And it was killing him.

"I guess the baby's not worried about timing," he said, and before he could get all the words out, Dylan's hold became a vise on his hand as another pain engulfed her.

He could barely stand the knowledge that she could have been going through all of this alone. If he hadn't come back, if he hadn't been up here with her when the power failure came— He cut off those thoughts with another: If he hadn't ever left, she might have been in a hospital getting all the help she needed instead of being stranded up here with a man who didn't know what to do for her.

"Oh, Coop," she breathed. "The towel."

He reached for a wet towel and held it to her forehead, then her cheeks. She sank back into the makeshift pillows he'd made from towels and tried to take easy breaths. "How about Shakespeare, if it's a boy?"

"Sure. And Suess if it's a girl."

"I was thinking of—"

Her hold on him convulsed when another wave of pain came, and as he watched her, he could see she was exhausted. He had a sudden fear that she might not be able to make it. God, she seemed so fragile and vulnerable, yet she wasn't complaining. And he didn't know how early "too early" was for a child. Towels were draped over her legs, her dress was up around her middle and her whole body was soaked with perspiration from the labor and the heat in the room.

"I...told Tori that they didn't call this labor for nothing." She rubbed her stomach over and over again. "I owe her an apology when—"

She gasped as the contraction came, and he held her hand, willing her to make it. He had so much to lose now, that it shook him. He could lose Dylan. He could lose the child. God, it hurt. It was a physical pain in his middle that seemed to tear through him.

He braced himself with one hand and leaned close to her, close enough to look into her eyes as the pain started to fade. "Dylan, you can do it. You're doing great. Hang on. The lights will be on soon. Then we can get help."

Her hand touched his face, and he could feel the way she was trembling. Despite the heat, she'd felt cold for the last ten minutes. "It's too late," she whispered hoarsely.

"No, people take hours to have babies," he said, but he didn't know how she could go on like this much longer.

"Oh, no," she gasped as another pain came, but this time she wasn't arching back. She moved as if to sit up, but didn't. She grabbed her knees and gasped for air over and over again, then she fell back into the towels.

"Dylan, just relax, love. Please, just try and relax."

"It's coming, Coop, it—" Another pain came, and Coop put his arm behind Dylan's neck and shoulders to try to support her until the pain began to ease and she leaned back. As she collapsed into the towels again, she cried, "I have to push, and I don't know if I should."

She licked her lips. "Tori…she said you can't push if it's too early, but if I don't push…" Tears came, and Coop felt his own eyes burn.

He didn't know how it could be too early to push with the way her pains were going, almost overlapping each other, and he took a deep breath, then said words that he prayed were right. "It's time, love, just push. I think the baby's ready to come out and meet its mother and father."

Before she could say anything, another pain came, and Coop grabbed more towels. One thing he knew was that the baby needed to be warm when it came out. That, and it had to cry. He pushed more towels behind Dylan so she could stay up higher, then took more towels and was going to put them under her hips. But when he looked, he froze. In the dimness he could see something; he realized it was the baby's head.

He got to his knees, and the pain excruciating but nothing compared to what Dylan was enduring. He ignored it, laid towels on the carpet, and then, without taking his eyes off the baby's head, he said, "It's coming. That's it. It's coming." The pains ran into each other, and he heard Dylan take a gasp of air, before bearing down again.

Suddenly a pure miracle happened. The head was there, then one shoulder, another, and he had barely reached for the baby before it slid out into his hands. He looked at his child—his daughter—still attached by the cord. But she wasn't moving.

"Coop, Coop," Dylan said. "Is it all right?"

He acted instinctively, doing things he didn't even know he knew he should do until that moment. He took her by her tiny feet and lifted her up and out until she was upside down, then he gently tapped her fragile back. And all the time he was praying, over and over and over again, that his little girl would breathe and cry.

If only he could see, if only he could see how she looked, what her coloring was. Then another miracle happened. The side lights in the office flickered and came back on. He must have hit the switch while he was rushing to get things. Now there was light.

And he was looking at his daughter—a tiny, messy little person hanging limply from his hands with her skin ominously blue tinged. He could sense Dylan struggling to get up. Just when he thought everything was lost, he felt a shuddering and the next moment, the baby cried. It was a tentative sound, but after another shudder, it grew louder and louder.

"Thank God," he breathed.

"The cord," Dylan said. "Use the string you found in the cupboards and tie it off."

He moved quickly, laying the baby on a towel at Dylan's feet, moving by rote, trying not to think until the crying baby was freed. Then he grabbed a towel, awkwardly wrapping her in it, and as her cries grew stronger, her color started to turn pink.

He looked down into her tiny face, contorted and wrinkled, and he saw a beauty that all but broke his heart.

"Coop?"

He managed to get back around Dylan, then eased the baby into her arms. "A girl. Our daughter."

As she cradled the baby, Coop sank back, trying to stretch his leg out, but he never took his eyes off Dylan or the child. Dylan was soaked, her hair plastered to her head and face, her skin pale and delicate looking. One of the baby's feet was free of the towels—a foot so tiny it looked as if it could belong to a doll, a doll that was crying at the top of her lungs now.

Dylan glanced at Coop, her tears silent and shimmering on her cheeks, and he felt a connection with her that drew him like a magnet into the circle that the three of them now formed. Then she looked away, tugged at her tangled dress and offered the baby her breast. The baby squirmed, twisting toward her mother, rooting into the heat. Then suddenly the crying stopped. As Dylan held the baby to her, Coop reached out to touch the exposed foot.

It was tiny and warm. "Perfect."

"Oh, yes," Dylan breathed.

He met her navy blue gaze. "We did it, love. We did it."

"It's that moment, isn't it?" she asked on a weak whisper. "When everything's perfect?"

"This is it," he said, knowing how true that was.

She looked down at the baby nursing at her breast. "Oh, yes, it is."

The adrenaline, or whatever it was that had carried him through the delivery, was draining from Coop. The discomfort in his leg had gone beyond simple pain to knifing agony, and it felt as if his whole leg was on fire.

A soft chiming sound startled him, and it took him a second to realize it was the sound of the elevator stopping on this floor. He forced himself to stand; the pain was starting to encompass every cell of his being. Grabbing the chair, he steadied himself, then looked down at Dylan. "Someone's here," he managed. "A bit late, but—"

"I know the old saying," she replied weakly with the shadow of a smile. "Better late than never."

"I love you," he said, then turned and nearly dragged himself across to the door.

By the time he got to the outer office, the guard from downstairs was coming into the room. He looked shocked to see Coop—his eyes widened and his hand automatically went to his waist for the gun there.

"What in the hell— What's going on up here?" he demanded.

It was then that Coop looked down and saw the blood on his shirt and arms, and he realized how he looked. "We need help." Then he didn't know if it was the combination of the pain and the sight of the blood, but suddenly he was doing something that he'd never done before in his life. As the guard looked at him, Coop put out a hand. And before he could say more than, "She had the baby," he fainted dead away.

COOP WAS LYING on his back. Pain throbbed in his leg, and voices were coming at him. For a moment he thought he was back in the hospital in Spain. But when he heard "He just fainted, ma'am. Some of them do that," he knew exactly where he was.

"His leg . . . It's hurt. Be careful."

He'd fainted.

"Yes, ma'am, we'll check it."

He felt something being put under his sore leg and the pain started to ease almost immediately. Then another voice called, "I'd guess at six pounds."

"So, what's the birth time?"

He heard Dylan's voice again. "Whatever time the lights came back on, that's when she cried."

"Three o'clock exactly," someone said.

Coop eased his eyes open to bright light and men in green. Blinking to adjust to the glare, he tried to push himself up, but hands on him held him down. "Hold it there. Take it easy. Everything's going well. Mother and daughter are ready to go to the hospital.''

He looked at the man standing over him. "Get me up.''

"Sir."

"Just get me up," he demanded. All he wanted was to see Dylan and the baby, to see for himself that they were okay.

"Yes, sir," the paramedic said and helped Coop get to his feet. His leg felt almost numb now, and he grabbed the doorjamb to steady himself. When he saw Dylan, he felt his world settle. She'd been put on a stretcher and had the baby in her arms swaddled in a white sheet. Their eyes met, and he felt a connection that was staggering.

"Love" didn't begin to describe what he felt at that moment.

"You fainted," she said with the hint of a smile on her pale face.

"It's a first." He glanced at the baby lying quietly in her arms. "One of many tonight." At that moment, he felt a kind of peace that he'd never known before in his life. In a life where he'd never felt connected, where he'd never felt as if he had a home, where he'd never really cared about anyone beyond himself, he'd found his core, his roots and maybe his soul. Right here in this building, with Dylan.

"Mister, we have to get your wife and daughter to the hospital so they can be checked out."

His wife and daughter. Soon, he thought. "Where're you taking them?"

"To Community over near Balboa."

He didn't have a clue where that was, but he knew he wasn't letting her and the baby out of his sight. "I'll ride in the ambulance with them."

"You can drive yourself, if you feel well enough."

"I might faint again any minute," he said without batting an eye. "And I can't walk. My leg's pretty messed up."

"Oh. Well, okay, then let's get this show on the road. The traffic's rough since the blackout." The man called to another technician. "Get that wheelchair over here."

Coop was more than grateful to sit in the chair alongside Dylan, and as they were both pushed out the door into the hallway, he reached up and grabbed her hand.

They rode down in the elevator in silence, just holding on to each other. When they got out at the lobby and started for the doors, the guard called from across the lobby, "Hey, is everything all right?"

"Great," Coop called back to the man. "Just great."

"The little one—is it a boy or a girl?"

"A girl."

"What's her name?"

Coop looked at Dylan. "I guess Suess is out?"

"Way out. I was thinking more of my grandmother's name, Anna. But I haven't thought about a second name."

As the stretcher got to the front doors, Coop saw a sign that said, Welcome to the Santa Clare Building—part of San Diego's History.

"Her name is Anna Clare," he called to the man.

Dylan smiled at him, and he could see that she understood immediately. "Anna Clare," she said softly. "Perfect."

Halloween

"IT'S YOUR TURN."

"No, it's your turn."

"I did it the last time, so you do it this time."

"No, *I* did it last. You just dreamed you did, because I was letting you sleep."

"It wasn't a dream."

"My leg hurts."

"Your leg is as good as new."

"Residual discomfort."

"Are you going to faint?"

"Only if you promise to leave me where I fall and not disturb me until at least eight."

"That's pitiful."

"So is dreaming that you did your turn when you slept like a baby."

Dylan rolled onto her back in the darkened bedroom and felt the heat of Coop's body along her side. "Are you sure? I thought I nursed her at midnight."

He shifted. Then, as she opened her eyes, she found him supporting himself on one elbow and looking down at her in the shadows. "It's four and she was up at two. It's mealtime—again."

"She's over three months old. She should be sleeping through the night, don't you think?"

"Do babies ever sleep through the night?"

She touched his jaw, brushing the bristling of a new beard, and smiled up at her husband. "It's rumored that some do. Maybe the Halloween party was too much for her."

"Could be. Having to dress up like the Easter Bunny at her age must be hard to swallow."

"Oh, she looked cute."

Coop touched her lips with one finger. "Shh, listen."

"What?" she asked, listening to the soft patter of rain on the windowpanes—but no crying. "Do you think she's gone back to sleep?"

Coop leaned over Dylan and placed his lips where his finger had been. Then he drew back. "I sure do, and we're awake," he said in a rough whisper.

"Oh, Mr. Reeves, you come up with the best ideas."

"That's why I'm in the think tank at the company," he said.

"And why you let others try to kill themselves in the test cars." She faltered. "You don't miss that, do you?"

"I'd be lying if I said I never get an urge to get behind the wheel again and push it. But Brokaw's right. He always was. Only people who don't have anything to lose can do it and do it right. And I've got way too much to lose now—with you, soon to be famous for doing the new project near Coronado, and Anna Clare, already famous for being the best Easter Bunny ever."

She laughed, but the sound faltered from the intensity of her feelings. "I love you," she whispered and circled his neck with her arms, pulling him down to her.

They'd been married three days after the blackout—less than four months ago—but every time Coop touched her, Dylan felt as if it was the first. And when they kissed, when his body covered hers, a passion that grew each time came suddenly and completely.

There was an urgency between them, a need that consumed and overwhelmed, and when Coop touched her and filled her, she arched to him. Their movements, urgent and almost painfully needy, matched perfectly, and when the culmination came, Dylan felt whole and complete.

As they lay together in the shadows, Dylan burrowed into the feelings of happiness like a child with a favorite blanket—the heat of Coop, his hold on her, his hand on her stomach, his thigh over hers, his heart beating against her, and rain falling softly outside.

In the stillness, a cry sounded; Anna Clare was awake again. "The kid's got great timing," Coop murmured.

"The question is, who's going to get her?"

Coop shifted, dropped a quick kiss on Dylan's lips, then slipped away from her. She could see him moving through the shadows. His limp was almost gone, despite his complaints about his leg. He slipped on his jeans, then after a quick trip to the bathroom, he crossed the room to head for the nursery. "If she's hungry, she's all yours," he said as he left.

"Try to find a rerun of *Gilligan's Island.* That always puts her right to sleep," she called after him.

Dylan settled back in bed, lying very still. She could feel herself drifting off, and just when she was about to fall asleep, she heard something.

Music. Soft and low, but she recognized it right away. "You Send Me." And sleep was gone.

Dylan smiled as she slipped out of bed, put on her terry-cloth robe, then padded barefoot down the hallway. The nursery was empty, so she went toward the sound of the music coming from the front of the house.

She stopped at the arched entry to the living room when she saw Coop in the shadows, cradling the baby on his shoulder. He was dancing in slow, easy circles with Anna Clare in front of the fireplace, the only spot that wasn't cluttered with baby paraphernalia or her work equipment.

Dylan watched for a long moment, then went to her husband and child. When she touched his arm, his steps faltered for a moment, then Coop paused and leaned toward her. "She's almost asleep," he whispered.

She looked from her husband to Anna Clare, then put her arms around the two of them and pressed her head to Coop's shoulder. "No more lessons in living for the moment," she whispered. "I've got it down pat."

She felt Coop brush his lips on the top of her head. Then, as the music played softly all around, the three of them slowly danced in the dark.

BRIDE'S
BAY RESORT

UNLOCK THE DOOR TO GREAT ROMANCE AT BRIDE'S BAY RESORT

Join Harlequin's new across-the-lines series, set in an exclusive hotel on an island off the coast of South Carolina.

Seven of your favorite authors will bring you exciting stories about fascinating heroes and heroines discovering love at Bride's Bay Resort.

Look for these fabulous stories coming to a store near you beginning in January 1996.

Harlequin American Romance #613 in January
Matchmaking Baby by Cathy Gillen Thacker

Harlequin Presents #1794 in February
Indiscretions by Robyn Donald

Harlequin Intrigue #362 in March
Love and Lies by Dawn Stewardson

Harlequin Romance #3404 in April
Make Believe Engagement by Day Leclaire

Harlequin Temptation #588 in May
Stranger in the Night by Roseanne Williams

Harlequin Superromance #695 in June
Married to a Stranger by Connie Bennett

Harlequin Historicals #324 in July
Dulcie's Gift by Ruth Langan

Visit Bride's Bay Resort each month wherever Harlequin books are sold.

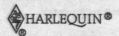

HARLEQUIN ®

HARLEQUIN®

Don't miss these Harlequin favorites by some of our most
distinguished authors!
And now, you can receive a discount by ordering two or more titles!

HT #25663	THE LAWMAN by Vicki Lewis Thompson	\$3.25 U.S. ☐/\$3.75 CAN. ☐
HP #11788	THE SISTER SWAP by Susan Napier	\$3.25 U.S. ☐/\$3.75 CAN. ☐
HR #03293	THE MAN WHO CAME FOR CHRISTMAS by Bethany Campbell	\$2.99 U.S. ☐/\$3.50 CAN. ☐
HS #70667	FATHERS & OTHER STRANGERS by Evelyn Crowe	\$3.75 U.S. ☐/\$4.25 CAN. ☐
HI #22198	MURDER BY THE BOOK by Margaret St. George	\$2.89 ☐
HAR #16520	THE ADVENTURESS by M.J. Rodgers	\$3.50 U.S. ☐/\$3.99 CAN. ☐
HH #28885	DESERT ROGUE by Erin Yorke	\$4.50 U.S. ☐/\$4.99 CAN. ☐

(limited quantities available on certain titles)

	AMOUNT	\$
DEDUCT:	10% DISCOUNT FOR 2+ BOOKS	\$
ADD:	POSTAGE & HANDLING	\$
	(\$1.00 for one book, 50¢ for each additional)	
	APPLICABLE TAXES**	\$
	TOTAL PAYABLE	\$
	(check or money order—please do not send cash)	

To order, complete this form and send it, along with a check or money order for the
total above, payable to Harlequin Books, to: **In the U.S.:** 3010 Walden Avenue,
P.O. Box 9047, Buffalo, NY 14269-9047; **In Canada:** P.O. Box 613, Fort Erie, Ontario,
L2A 5X3.

Name:_____

Address:_____ City:_____

State/Prov.:_____ Zip/Postal Code:_____

**New York residents remit applicable sales taxes.
  Canadian residents remit applicable GST and provincial taxes.   HBACK-JS3

Look us up on-line at: http://www.romance.net

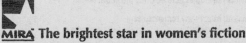

Sabrina   It Happened One Night
Working Girl   Pretty Woman
While You Were Sleeping

If you adore romantic comedies then have
we got the books for you!

Beginning in **August 1996** head to your
favorite retail outlet for
LOVE & LAUGHTER™,
a brand-new series with two books every
month capturing the lighter side of love.

You'll enjoy humorous love stories by favorite
authors and brand-new writers, including
JoAnn Ross, Lori Copeland, Jennifer Crusie,
Kasey Michaels, and many more!

As an added bonus—with the retail purchase,
of two new Love & Laughter books you can
receive a **free** copy of our fabulous
Love and Laughter collector's edition.

**LOVE & LAUGHTER™—a natural
combination...always
romantic...always entertaining**

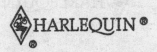

A baby was the last thing they were

But after nine months, the idea of fatherhood begins to grow on three would-be bachelors.

Enjoy three complete stories by some of your favorite authors—all in one special collection!

THE STUD by Barbara Delinsky
A QUESTION OF PRIDE by Michelle Reid
A LITTLE MAGIC by Rita Clay Estrada

Available this July wherever books are sold.

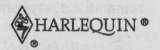

HARLEQUIN ®